GROWING UP

BOOK ONE

MATTLOCK LONDON

BOOKS

Printed in the United States of America
Antioch Books, LLC - Forney, TX

Hardcover ISBN 979-8-9859103-2-2
Paperback ISBN 979-8-9859103-1-5
Kindle ISBN 979-8-9859103-0-8
EPUB ISNB 979-8-9859103-3-9

Library of Congress Control Number: 2022904696

mattlocklondon.com
info@mattlocklondon.com

Published by Antioch Books, LLC

To my Sarah.
Thank you for believing in my dreams as much as I do. Thank you for your support, for keeping me grounded, for living this crazy adventurous life with me! I couldn't imagine doing any of this with anyone else. When I'm weak you're strong and when you're strong I'm weak. :)
Thank you for being my best friend.
Thank you for being my wife.
I love you more than I could ever say.

+

To my right hand throughout this project, Kalea Ellison. Your encouragement, help and most importantly your friendship mean the world to me. Thanks for all of your hard work with the edits, help with the revisions, rewrites and honestly helping me make sure I don't sound like a complete idiot!

Intro

WINTER 1993
MATTY

Maybe if I hold my breath he won't hear me. Okay, Matty, nice and calm. Deep breath in and hold it. How can I fix all of this? I'm just a 10-year-old girl! A 10-year-old girl that really messed things up.

We can hear the Monster in the front room, through our locked bedroom door. The Monster is wrecking everything, screaming at Mommy. I'm terrified and I can't help but show it. I'm shaking, like when you're really cold. But I'm not cold. I'm scared. I try and wedge myself in closer to Brother. That's what I call him, Brother. He's older than me and he's my hero. We're both hiding under his bed. He calls it "The Fortress of Solitude," like Superman's hideout. He wants to be Superman. He wants to be every superhero. I think he's better than all of them though. I feel much safer with him around.

The sound of glass breaking startles me in closer to Brother. We're being as quiet as we can. I'm trying not to breathe. Maybe the Monster will forget we're in the house. The noises coming from the front room sound like the Monster is winning. Poor Mom. I'd cry for her, but I'm so scared I can't even move.

Tonight is all my fault. If I had just listened to Brother. If I hadn't broken the Monster's tape case, he wouldn't have hurt Brother. He wouldn't be hurting Mom. I should have just listened. I should have just read my Barbie comics, or played with my dolls, or toys or something! Anything! I want to cry but I can't. My throat is tight like I'm fighting it back, but I'm not. I'm just so terrified that if I make a sound the Monster will find us!

The Monster hasn't always been the Monster. He turned into the Monster over time. He's the worst when he drinks beer. Nasty, nasty beer. He transforms, like the bad guys in Brother's comics. I guess some of the good guys transform too, but he's definitely not a good guy. He's the bad guy. He's the worst kind of bad guy. He hurts my Mom. He hurt my Brother.

My lungs are burning. I'm trying to hold my breath. More noise comes from the front room, pain-filled noise. We breathe with the bangs and crashes. If we let out the breath when the Monster wrecks stuff, he won't be able to hear us. Hopefully. I make sure I time my breaths with Brother. He looks over at me like he's going to ask a question. My eyes widen, my body tenses.

What could he want to know
right now? Don't ask anything!

"Did you say my name?" he whispers.

What? Why is he asking me that?

I look at him, obviously confused. I quickly glance toward the door to make sure the Monster isn't on his way in. Still closed. Still locked. I can't answer, I don't want to make a sound. I shake my head slightly in response. He's already making too much noise with all his whispering. Brother goes back to whatever it is he's thinking about. I don't know what to think about. Everything that's happening is so big, bigger than me: the Monster, Mom out there by herself, Brother hearing things.

Brother nudges me, "You say my name?"
I answer this time, "No!" It's louder than I intended it to be. What is happening?

Why does he keep asking me questions? Is he so scared that he's going crazy? Am I next? Will I start hearing voices too?

Brother grabs my hand, pulling me from my frantic thoughts. He starts crawling out from under the bed, dragging me behind him.

"What are we doing?!" I demand. We're leaving the safety of The Fortress! We are so much closer to the Monster! He needs to know I'm not okay with this!

"We're going to Bill and Felicia's house," he responds in a tone that lets me know there is no changing his mind. His face is set. He knows what he's doing. I don't know what's happening but if Brother is going, I'm going too. As we clear the bed and stand to our feet, I hesitate, immediately noticing that our bedroom door is wide open. Brother closed and locked it before we crawled under his bed. I know he did. Brother feels my hesitation and yanks my arm a little, urging me to get moving. There's no time to figure this out.

We start running.

ONE

***What's that smell?   Good
Lord! Mom is making French toast!***

Being forced to wake up from an awesome flying dream is not the way any twelve-year-old boy wants their Saturday morning to kick off.   But if I had to pick a forgivable reason, the smell of Mom cooking French toast would have to be on the list.

Once I realize Mom is making my favorite breakfast, I sit up so fast I almost fall right out of bed. Whew! From flying to falling! I was not ready for that! It's kind of like that dream that you have when you're falling and you jerk yourself awake and nearly poop yourself at the same time. After taking a few seconds to clear my head, I cautiously swing my legs over the side of my bed and reach my arms to the ceiling for a good stretch.

***Geez, I feel like a 98-year-
old Grandpa! With wrinkles, a walker***

*and everything! What the heck?!
Let's see... Bike to school, spaghetti
from the cafeteria - that couldn't be it
- could it? - Nah! Haha! After
school, we biked home. Oh, wait!
Seaver Park Hill. Yep. How could I
have forgotten that we rolled down
that hill at least a hundred times?
And now I'm a Grandpa. Thanks a
lot, Seaver Park Hill! I'm too young
to be 98!*

I look across the room and immediately notice my little sister, Matty's bed is not only empty, it's made. She's already awake? I wonder what time it is and how on earth she managed to wake up, make her bed and exit without waking me. I must have been in a deep sleep. I have a bad habit of reading comics under my X-Men blankets with a flashlight. Even after Mom has already called for lights out.

All right, it's time to just suck it up and get out of bed. I have already lingered for too long. Another bad habit. I close my eyes, take a deep breath and stand up. I turn and do my best to straighten my bed. About as good as any 12-year-old 98-year-old would do. My mind isn't totally committed anyway. I wonder if Mom has gotten to the laundry yet. Today feels like a Power Rangers shirt kind of day. I'm about to have French toast for breakfast *and* it's Saturday.

As I flip through the shirts in my closet, it becomes quite obvious that Mom has not yet gotten to the laundry and it indeed is *not* "Morphin' Time." Oh well! I reach for the next best thing: my Ghostbusters shirt. This is not your average, everyday, run-of-the-mill Ghostbusters shirt, mind you. This one glows in the dark! This shirt makes people jealous. Really jealous. That could be why I like it so much.

I've lingered long enough, again. I pull on my really cool shirt that makes people jealous, step into my jeans, throw on some socks and shoes, and head out to face the day!

As per usual, when I open my door into the living room, the sound of music fills the house. The Steve Miller Band is playing a private concert just for us from the kitchen radio. I round the corner and there she is: My Mom, dancing and singing into the spatula as if she's just been handed the mic. She's definitely trying to impress.

My mom is a model of a woman. She turns heads wherever she goes. She isn't a very big woman - not short. Just… petite? I think that's what you call it. What she lacks in size, she makes up for in energy. She has to in order to be a single mom to two kids like us. Mom has wavy, brown hair that looks great in any style. In the winter she likes to grow it long and she cuts it above her shoulders in the summer.

Mom dances a massive plate of French toast over to the table and gives me a look I recognize immediately. She gives us this look often.   The look that says, "Good morning. I love you. Don't talk to me until this song is over."   I know better than to challenge her on this one. Besides, I like The Steve Miller Band.

I take a seat across from Matty at the kitchen table. She is completely lost in a game of Tetris (on *my* Gameboy, mind you). I can hear her frantically rotating the different blocks. Admittedly, the look of panic on her face is a little entertaining. It brings a grin to my face. I know, I know - it's different when you're the one playing. You've never known real stress until you've gotten yourself backed up to only two rows to move around in and it's your last life. Man. If only things stayed that simple.

"What level you on?" I ask.
"I can't talk!" she barks, "I have to concentrate!"
"Sounds like-" I'm interrupted by the sound of her last life slipping right through her fingers. Game over. She dramatically drops the Gameboy to the table.   Her arms droop to her sides as she slowly lifts her eyes to mine. She takes in a deep breath and then starts, as usual, to give what I know will be some arbitrary reason as to why she didn't win. It's more than likely my fault this time, naturally.

"See what you made me do? I was about to beat the high score!"

No, she wasn't. Not even close. I forever hold the high score. I know this because I check daily. Have to stay on top! Back to Matty though. She once blamed the sound of the air conditioner turning on for her failing miserably in some other game. Once she even blamed the fact that she had to blink. Which means she was desperately trying not to blink! Hilarious! I try to call her out on these types of things regularly.

I grin at Matty. She shoots a snotty look back at me. Mom finally joins us at the table. She pauses for just a moment to look at all the food on the table, then at us, and smiles.

> ***There's literally enough French toast here to feed the entire town! Challenge accepted!***

I make it my duty to eat an impressive amount (or a shameful amount - depends on how you look at it). I begin to build my mountain of toast, piling on one slice after another. Once I'm sure I have an impressive amount, I reach for the syrup to pour on the river of maple deliciousness.

"Why don't you just start with two or three pieces and not 102 or three?" Mom asks playfully. As fun-loving as she is, she really knows how to get through to me. Even when she's being silly, her words carry weight. Mom has a way with discipline that never really feels like discipline. She's great!

Dad left a while back.   Matty doesn't really remember, but I do. At first, I didn't understand, then I was sad. After that, I moved on to being angry, but something inside me helped me just let it all go. I feel fine now. I know Mom worries about me sometimes. Every once in a while she looks at me with this sad expression and I wish I can put her mind at ease. Mom is awesome. She loves us so much. Sometimes Matty and I wonder if she loves us *too* much. She tells us like every day! And today is no different.

"I love you two," she says from across the table.
"WE KNOW!" we say in unison.
As we devour our food like it'll run away if we don't eat it fast enough, mom asks, "So you guys have big plans today?"
"We're gonna go hang out with the guys," I say with my mouth full. Mom doesn't like it when we talk with our mouths full, but I don't have a choice! My mouth has to stay full if I'm going to get out of here in time. If she really wants an answer, then food will be involved.

Matty is still pouting that her dreams of beating my high score were dashed. Although, it didn't slow her eating any.   That girl can put away some French toast!   Well honestly, she can just pack away food in general.

"You guys gonna be bustin' some ghosts?" Mom asks, pointing to my shirt.
"What? Oh… Maybe? I dunno." I cram the last of Mt. Toast into my mouth and rise to my feet.

"Geez. You wanna let that settle a little?" Mom asks with slight concern in her voice.

"No time, Mom! Too much to do!" I answer as I run off, Matty calling after me.

"Wait!" She shoves what she can in her mouth and races in behind.

Matty and I burst out the front door and run to our bikes parked on the sidewalk just off the front porch. I throw my leg over my bike and "start it up" like you would a motorcycle. Yes, I make all the motions and noises. It's no fun if you don't commit! Matty copies me and "starts up" her bike as well. She usually does everything I do. It never really bothers me though. We've always been close. Always will be.

Out of all of our friends, Charles lives the closest to us. It works out perfectly because his house is the midway point from everyone else's. The crew usually meets there. The ride to his house isn't bad at all. Mom's friends, Bill and Felicia are outside doing some yard work. They are an interesting pair, but they seem perfect for each other. Bill is in his 40's with a blonde mullet, a blonde beard and piercing blue eyes. He's always talking about feng shui, zen and stuff like that. Felicia has caramel brown skin that hints towards a Mediterranean ancestry and she keeps her dark hair in a pixie cut. Like Bill, she's also in her 40's and always says she's the "yin to his yang" because she's so bubbly and energetic. Matty calls their names and waves. She's definitely the more social of the two of us.

After passing their house, we have to be a lot more careful. A few houses down from Bill and Felicia's house lives Stupid Dog. That probably isn't its name, but that's what we call it. Stupid Dog is the worst. It's like it has something to prove. Every time we ride by its house it rockets off its front porch at full speed, barking its stupid head off.

Preparing myself to pass this house is no easy feat. Lots of deep breaths and talking myself up. I try all that mind-over-matter crap. You know how they say dogs can smell fear? Well, I'm doing all I can to make sure that devil dog doesn't smell fear on me, which I guess is always pretty easy to do. We rarely pass that house without me feeling the urge to crap my pants. Just so you know, I've never given in to that urge.

> *And here we go! Stupid Dog! What is it with this dog? Every time we ride past this house it loses its mind! Wait... come to think of it... I don't think it does this when we walk by. It just sits up there with its stupid little eyes looking at us, staring at us like we're peasants or something. It sits there daring us to get on our bikes and ride by so it can freak out.*
>
> *STUPID DOG HATES BIKES!*

RIGHT, LEFT, RIGHT, LEFT, ALMOST THERE!

I let out a heavy sigh of relief just as Stupid Dog gives up and trots back up to the porch to resume its day of stupidity. It just dawned on me that I've been holding my breath the entire chase! I hate that dog.

Next up is the stop sign the bus driver ran into. We call it the Sunshine Stop Sign. As we ride past the stop sign I reminisce about that crazy day the rest of the way.

The bus driver's name was Miss Sunshine. Don't let the name fool you. She was anything *but* sunshine. She wasn't sunny or shiny, or anything that resembled the two words. I honestly think she just enjoyed yelling at kids. It didn't help that Jeremy Leaf rode the bus. He was literally the loudest human being that I've ever encountered in my entire life. Even his breathing was loud. It didn't make all

that much sense because he wasn't very big. He was just…
so loud.

> *I bet he has some kind of condition. That kid is always standing. Always. Maybe he has a condition that makes it impossible to bend his knees… and for some reason makes him extremely loud. That's got to be it. His condition makes it impossible to talk at a normal volume and bend his knees. Gotta be it. Only way it makes sense.*

So there we were, riding on the bus, Jeremy doing his thing, being loud. Miss Sunshine was having none of it. You could always tell when Miss Sunshine was about to yell. There was a build-up. First, her fingers would begin tapping rapidly on the steering wheel. Then she would inhale deeply and exhale loudly from her nose *and* throat. It was more of a growl. Actually, it was a strange combination of a heavy sigh and a growl. It was a *gr-igh*? Maybe it was a *s-rowl*? Anyway, before you knew it, she would pound the steering wheel with a balled up fist and explode. This time she turned around to yell at Jeremy Leaf, (which was usually the case), but this time she swerved and ran right into the stop sign! She didn't hit it directly, but it definitely scraped down the side of the bus. Everyone screamed in terror, which caused Miss Sunshine to yell out in anger even more. For some reason, instead of just driving straight through, past the sign, she slammed the bus in reverse and started backing up.

Jeremy Leaf, being the strange, loud kid that he was, wanted to get a better look, so he stuck his head out the window. As the stop sign scraped down the side of the bus for the second time, Jeremy noticed the sign was headed straight for his face. Instead of pulling his head back in like any normal person would, he started screaming. Just screaming. Everything was *so loud*! The scraping of metal on metal, every kid screaming, Jeremy screaming, Miss Sunshine screaming… it was bad. One of Jeremy's idiot friends managed to pull him back in just before he lost his head.

Once we were clear of the stop sign, you'd think the bus driver would stop the bus and hop back on the road. Nope. Not Miss Sunshine. She just kept backing up. Right into the ditch on the other side of the road! The bus even tipped back for a moment. Of course, that caused everyone to scream even more. Those that weren't screaming from fear were the psychopaths, Leaf and his idiots, trying to get the bus to teeter-totter. Did I mention it was loud? So loud. That was the last day Matty and I rode the bus.

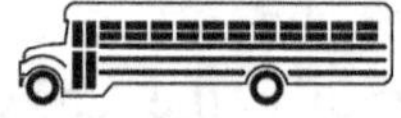

Before I know it, we've pulled up to Charles' two-story house and, as expected, the whole crew is here. All of their bikes litter the front yard. Matty and I follow suit, lazily dropping our bikes in the grass among the others.

It's odd how memories that span a long amount of time connect and they all just seem so close together. One event after another. Kind of like dominoes.

TWO

Matty and I park our bikes on the lawn with the rest of the bikes and make our way to the door. I knock a couple of times and the door opens. Charles greets us with a chocolate-covered grin.   He says "hello" with his eyebrows since his mouth is otherwise occupied with a doughnut. Charles hasn't hit his growth spurt yet, so he's shorter than most kids our age, but he's built like an athlete. He's Native American, Cherokee, with dark hair parted down the middle. Charles also tends to be a little too confident for his own good. He motions for us to enter and we walk in like it's our second home. Which it kind of is! His mom and dad are at the kitchen table reading the newspaper and drinking coffee.

"Hey, Mr. and Mrs. Hughes!" I yell as we run upstairs to Charles' room.

I try to be polite. Not that I'm rude or anything, I just forget manners sometimes. I'm usually in my own mind with whatever story I'm cooking up. I have a pretty vivid imagination.

"Good morning!" They yell after us, but we're already gone.

Charles leads us to his room where the rest of the gang are already deep in the zone. Maps are spread out all over Charles' bed with walkie-talkies and all kinds of fake weaponry being readied. As Matty and I arrive in the doorway, everyone stops what they're doing and turns to face us, all smiles. We're all here, all five of us. Our crew is inseparable. We are the model and exact definition of best friends.

First up, my literal best friend in the entire universe, Tommy. Tommy's parents are an interracial couple. His mom is Caucasian and his dad is Hispanic. Tommy has light brown skin, brown eyes and dark brown curly hair. One of his curls is always hanging down on his forehead like Superman or Michael Jackson. I've often wondered if he does this on purpose or his hair just kind of… does it. I've never asked though. Maybe I will someday when it seems right. Tommy has the life, man. His mom is the manager at McDonald's, which means he gets all the really cool Happy Meal toys! ALL OF THEM! Sometimes he lets Matty and me in on it.

Then there's Jason. He introduced me to the Ghostbusters, for which I will forever be grateful. He is a tall, lanky blonde kid with a chili-bowl haircut. If you don't know what that is, be grateful. Just imagine your mom placing a big bowl on your head like a helmet, then chopping off whatever hair hangs below the bowl. I'm pretty sure that is exactly what his mom does. I got a chili-bowl cut once and it was bad. Brutal. Jason also has a really weird obsession with Elvis Presley. We all think it's weird. His extra-long arms and legs are a sight to see when he does his Elvis dance moves. We can't figure out why he loves Elvis so much when there's Michael Jackson and Guns N Roses.

At first, before he joined our group, I really, really didn't like Charles. It wasn't because he claimed he had every available gaming console there was. It was because he told us he could do the cool slide that Sub Zero does in the game Mortal Kombat. I didn't believe he could do it then and I still don't believe he can now. He will never show us! Is it really so unreasonable to ask for proof?

"I can only do it when I'm fighting, and I'd never fight one of you guys!"

Bunch of bullcrap, if you ask me. In all honesty, I'm jealous. Even though I don't believe him, deep down I want to be the one in the group that can do the Sub Zero slide. We mostly call him Charles, but if he does something that really irks me I call him Chuck. I don't want to insult him, he's my friend, but calling him Chuck… that's about the most demeaning thing I can let myself do to him. It makes me think of up-chuck or throw-up… which makes me feel nauseated if I think about it too much. I guess that does me just as much harm. Regardless, it gets the point across!

Next up in our group is my sister, Matty, the youngest of us all. She's two years younger than me and one year younger than everyone else. We're siblings so we have a lot of similarities when it comes to our looks. We both have brown hair, except hers is long and wavy. We both have a lighter complexion that darkens in the summer and dark brown eyes. Matty is petite like Mom, but don't let that fool you. She's powerful! She's pretty too. Matty's cool. All the others think so too. She's the most adventurous of us all!

Now, finally, me! I'm the oldest of the group. I should be an entire grade higher than the guys and two grades higher than Matty, but I had to go to a "special" class before I even started 1st grade. They said I wasn't ready because of my attention span. I have "an overactive imagination" or something like that. I couldn't focus. It's not my fault that they were boring, and so what if I always create scenarios in my mind? Everything is a movie after all. Everything is a scene. Life is just a story that's being played out!

"Bout time!" says Tommy with a huge grin splattered across his face. He tosses me a walkie. "We're trying to figure out an escape from Cry Baby Road."
"Wait. What?" My eyebrows can't help but shoot straight up.
"We're doin it," Tommy continues. "Today is the day we ride it. All the way through."

Jason looks up, matter of fact, pulls a red marker from his mouth like it's a cigar. "We're gonna take the proton packs and trap just in case. If *she* shows up, we'll catch her. We'll be heroes. They'll have a parade in our honor."

I like the sound of that. A parade. I'll wave, maybe throw out a little candy.   Only one glaring problem. Legend says Cry Baby Road is haunted and that anyone that goes down the road, day or night, never comes back out.   Some say that the road just never ends, it keeps stretching and stretching. You spend the rest of your life seeing the end but never getting there.   Some say that a Lady Ghost, the one Jason is referring to, haunts the road and keeps anyone that enters locked away for all of eternity.

One other hurdle. I hate to be the one to bring it up, but it seems like I'm the only one arriving to this particular information.   "Jason, we've never successfully trapped a ghost. We've never even seen one."

A silent moment passes, everyone deep in thought.

"Gotta start sometime!" Jason finally erupts. We all agree. In all honesty, we would never voice how we all truly feel. I mean the deep down feel, the real feel. The only truly brave one is Matty. And the only reason she's been silent is because, somehow, she has managed to get her hands on a doughnut like the one Charles had. Even after all that French toast, she's still going at it! Tommy rises to his feet, takes in a deep breath and announces, "Gear up everyone. We ride in 5!"

The October air feels fantastic! October is the best month, in my opinion. How can you deny Halloween?! The one time a year you can dress up in a crazy costume and no one even cares! In fact, people give you candy for doing it! Genius!

We're ready. Each of us is decked out in Ghostbusters gear. Never once have any of us brought up the fact that there are only 4 Ghostbusters and there are 5 of us. It doesn't matter. The 5 of us are a team no matter what. Once we reach the front yard, we line up our bikes, proton packs strapped to our backs. I take one solid look down the line to my left, Matty and Charles. I take one solid look down the line to my right, Tommy and Jason. I take in a deep breath and do my best Optimus Prime, "Autobots! Roll out!"

"ROLL OUT!" everyone chants in unison.

We race through the streets like they belong to us. I mean, why wouldn't they? We are literally about to save this town from the clutches of whatever haunts Cry Baby Road! We are heroes! We are champions! We do, however, ride the opposite way from Stupid Dog's house. We don't have the time or patience for all of that.

"Let's stop at The Shop on the way back!" Charles yells as we pass the storefront.

We all nod in agreement. The Comic Shop, or The Shop, was usually the first stop of Saturday mornings. We're regulars. The hill after The Comic Shop ends with a stoplight, which is a bummer because that means we can't coast at full speed. We have to stop at the light. Heroes should be law-abiding citizens and all. We ride hard and whip our bikes to the side as we brake. It seems like the cool thing to do. Now, at the light, looking at each other, we wait for the go-ahead to cross. The eternal crossing light.

"I wonder what's happening in Reign of Supermen this issue," Charles says.

Tommy looks at Charles, furrowed brow present, "You think it'll sell out?"

With heavy hesitation, I speak up, "What if we save the world after we get the comics? I mean, the Ghost will still be there."

> *Oh, man. I hope they don't think I'm a chicken with that suggestion.*

"Cool." Jason turns his bike back. Everyone follows suit. Sweet relief.

> *Boy am I glad that worked out. I'm honestly not ready to face Cry Baby Road, at least not yet. And of course, I could never say that out*

We slug up the hill about halfway and then we get off and push our bikes the rest of the way. It happens that way every time. I've made it the furthest up the hill, but still not all the way. It's a massive hill.

"I'm glad we decided to stop first! Barbie is taking a turn that I wasn't expecting!" Matty says with new excitement.

The rest of us groan in unison, "Barbie! Oh, come on!"

Matty is equal parts tomboy and girly-girl. I love moments like these. Opportunities to poke fun. I see it and I take it.

"So what? Barbie get an accidental perm or somethin'?"

"No!" Matty barks back.

"Have y'all ever smelled a perm?" I ask through everyone's chuckles. I'm now opening the floor to the rest of the guys. None of them have. "I'm telling the truth when I say it smells like a burning turd."

The group erupts with laughter. Jason takes his turn to poke fun. At me this time, "And how do you know what a burning turd smells like?"

We all laugh as we stroll into The Comic Shop's parking lot. We park our bikes and enter.

"Morning kids!"

"Morning Fred!" we answer back.

Fred's cool. He's a dude that owns a comic shop! What else could you want in life? Fred is tall and slim but has this strangely round belly. Probably from drinking too much pop or something. He has long, thick black hair and a light complexion. He always has a baseball cap resting on top of his head with his hair bursting out from under it and hiding all parts of his face except his smile. It's almost like he's trying to be like Slash from Guns N Roses. Fred is always wearing some kind of nerdy t-shirt and jeans with holes in the knees. Today he went with cut-off jean shorts. Now get this: The Comic Shop is the name of the store, and yes there are comics, but there is so much more! There are action figures and collectibles, there are games, there's candy and junk food. It's the place I want to call home. Fred has it made.

We make a line straight for the new releases. We grab what we came for immediately (to avoid the impending doom of the dreaded sell-out, of course) and as usual, we shuffle through some of the other titles. Something across the aisle catches my eye.

Oh, sweet Lord!   It's the friggin' Batmobile from Batman the Animated Series!

You know how in romance movies where some girl is running towards some guy in slow motion and the screen is all hazy like you've got something in your eyes? And how that's supposed to mean they're in love or something? That happened with me and the Batmobile. Well, not the exact same thing, but as close as one can get in real life. I'm in love. What do I know though? I'm a kid. I don't realize it, but apparently Matty has been saying my name for quite some time because she smacks me on the arm to snap me out of my daze.

"What was that for?!" I demand.
"Do you have $2.50?" she asks, annoyed.

She has a laugh at my expense as I dig in my pocket. I hand her a wad of bills and she skips off happily. Buying the latest Barbie Comic, I'm sure. Just gotta see what she does next! Good grief. Charles steps up, bag in hand. My gaze is still fixed on the Batmobile.

"Why don't you marry it?" Charles teases.
"Shut up Chuck!" My defense is weak. He knows it. I know it. I realize it's weird that I just had a "moment" with the Batmobile, but what can I do? There's a song that says something about not being able to help falling in love... or something like that. I think I'm beginning to understand. I have to get out of here before any other weirdness can happen.

Outside we sit on the curb and thumb through *Reign of the Supermen* while devouring candy. Jason bought a massive grab bag of junk food. I toss a snack-sized candy bar in my mouth and turn to Tommy.

"Cry Baby Road?"

Tommy grins.

THREE

Staring down Cry Baby Road, every one of us silent, all I can muster up is, "Seems like a normal road to me."

It doesn't seem like anyone else shares my thoughts since no one responds. All of a sudden, Matty scares the crap out of us all when she yells, "LET'S GOOOOO!!!"

Matty thrusting herself forward on her bike somehow thrusts us all forward. Like we are all tethered together by an invisible chain or rope. We rocket down Cry Baby Road as if we are riding actual motorcycles. Yelling at the top of our lungs, we blast out the other end of the road and brake sideways on our bikes. With the adrenaline flowing like a river, I turn and look to my crew, proud. We're all smiles. Well, everyone except Jason, who has managed to pull his Particle Accelerator from his back and is aiming it down the road like the ghost could emerge at any moment.

"We did it!" Tommy exclaims as he gives me a high five, "I ain't afraid of no ghost!"

We ride a little taller back through town. We've just defeated Cry Baby Road. No one else in history has accomplished what we just accomplished. We've done something no one else could! If any ghosts were haunting that road, they must have decided that we were the bigger threat and surrendered. Never to return. We have to celebrate. But how?

"We should get pizza!" I blurt out, high on adrenaline.

"Dude!" Jason swerves and nearly wrecks his bike at the suggestion. "I was literally *just* thinking that! You think we have powers now that we defeated the ghost? Did we level up?"

Matty, ever the voice of reason, "That's dumb. We're just hungry."

"I could get my mom to give us some Happy Meals," Tommy suggested. The next best thing. No one argues. We all turn and ride toward McDonald's. We deserve a victor's meal. We deserve that parade Jason mentioned earlier, but we'll settle for chicken nuggets and a toy.

We roll into the restaurant parking lot like we own the place. I mean, come on - we just saved the town. Plus Tommy's mom is the manager of one of the finest eating establishments in the entire known world. We park our bikes and walk in. Tommy walks up to the counter and says something to the worker at the register. Probably, "Can you get my mom", or something like that. I don't know, I'm not paying much attention. I'm dreaming of nuggets and barbeque sauce!

Moments later Tommy's mom steps through, smiles and waves. "I know what you guys are here for!"

We thank her. Heroes must always remember to be polite. We make our way to a booth, unload all of our gear in the booth behind us and take a seat. Feels good to sit down on a seat other than a bike. I'm grateful for the seat on the bike and all, but they definitely don't make those seats for comfort.

Tommy leans forward, stone-faced, "Not a word to my Mom about Cry Baby Road."

We all put the tips of our right thumbs and index fingers together and slowly drag an imaginary zipper closed across our lips, lock it up and throw away the key. The symbol of complete secrecy.

Tommy's mom appears with two heaping trays of Happy Meals, chocolate milk and every condiment a kid could ever want or need. And -

OH, DEAR LORD! The toys! It's Batman the Animated Series!

I quickly grab the box handed me, shout out a quick, "Thank you," pop the tabs and dig around for my toy. Batman! Awesome! I quickly turn my attention to everyone else.

"Who'd ya'll get?!" I'm anxious to know who got which toy.

Jason turns with a mouth full of fries and Charles is busy attempting to open his Sweet and Sour packet. I can't take it!

How in the world can they not be as excited about this as I am?

"I've got the Riddler," calls Tommy. He holds the unopened toy up for everyone to see. No one cares who Tommy got. We all know he'll end up getting all the toys anyway.

Matty perks up in excitement, "CATWOMAN!" She holds the toy up like it's the key to a secret door that holds all her heart's desires. At least that's the way it looks to me.

"Charles! Jason! Who do you have?!" I demand. It's ludicrous that I even need to ask!

"Oh," responds Charles as he finally turns his attention to find his toy.

That does it. "*Oh*?!" These are Batman toys, *Chuck*!"

> *Wow. That's two "Chucks" in one day. Maybe I'm being too hard on him?*

Charles continues to dig around in his box, unphased. Meanwhile, Jason discovers a Batman in his.

"I got Batman," Jason delivers.
"Same as me!" I respond excitedly.

> *Am I too excited about this? No. They aren't excited enough! I mean, Matty is just as stoked as I am, and Tommy seems to be right there with me even though… we all know he has all of these toys in the bank! Why isn't Jason as jazzed as I am? And* ***WHAT IS TAKING CHARLES SO LONG TO FIND HIS TOY?!***

"I got the same as Tommy," Charles finally reveals.
"The Riddler!" Tommy grins as he holds up his toy.
"Yup." Charles couldn't care less. He loads his mouth with more fries.
I turn to Tommy immediately. "Do they have the Batmobile?"
Tommy takes a bite of a chicken nugget just before I ask, so now I have to wait for the answer.

> *Great.   I had to wait on*
> *Charles and now I have to wait on*
> *Tommy.*

He smiles and then swallows his food.
"They do." He says, matter-of-fact.
My eyes widen.
"Not sure what week it comes out, though," he continues.

And with that, he crushes me. I fell in love earlier in The Comic Shop, but love was just out of reach at thirty dollars.   Now the glimmer of hope that sprang from a Happy Meal has been robbed from me as well.

"You'll get it next time!" Matty chums.

She's always so hopeful. The glass-half-full type. I don't think I'm necessarily a negative thinker, just sometimes half-full means the same thing as half-empty to me. I think they call that a realist, even though I often live in a dream world.

"Yeah, I'll ask my mom when they are supposed to come out." Tommy casually interrupts my thoughts.

And just like that, hope has returned. I'm satisfied with that answer. If I know the week of release I can carefully plan my strategy of how to procure my treasure! I turn my attention to my food now.

We plow through our nuggets, cheeseburgers, fries and chocolate milk. Afterward, we sit and let everything settle, silent. We've already had a very eventful day.

"What's next everybody?" I ask, feeling content.

Usually, we'd spend the morning out messing around, playing with toys, reading comics or playing video games. Then we'd watch the Saturday morning cartoons that Tommy's Grandparents always taped for us. Man, Tommy has the life!

"I'm going out of town with my Grandparents in a couple of hours," Tommy explains.

> ***Dang it Tommy! You're sending me on an emotional roller coaster today!***

"So we'll have to watch toons tomorrow or somethin'," he finishes.
"I have to help my dad clean out the garage," Jason informs. "Probably should get back. He'll be mad if I stay out too long."

That's two down. Maybe Matty, Charles and I can still do something. The Three Musketeers! The Three Amigos!

Charles chugs the last of his chocolate milk and then delivers the death blow. "My cousins are coming to visit from Texas, so I can't do anything for the rest of the day."

Well crap. What started out as the craziest, most fun day of my life has just screeched to a halt, and it's only noon!

What the heck am I gonna do now? I guess I could go home and play with toys. I could make sure my high score is still untouched in Tetris. Matty's gonna be busy with that Barbie comic, I just know it. Okay, okay. I'll just have to wing it. I'll be fine. We'll do toons tomorrow. All is well.

"Okay. Toons tomorrow," I say, accepting my fate. Everyone blasts, "Toons tomorrow!"

We do that kind of thing all the time. One of us will say something and the rest of us follow in unison like it empowers us or something. Like those words are our motto or creed or catchphrase. We think it's cool.

We gather our trash onto the trays and dump it all in the garbage bins. Afterward, we do our best to wipe down our booth from any spilled ketchup or mess we may have made and strap our gear back on. I pocket my

Batman and Matty hands me her Catwoman so I can do the same for her. She can stick something in her pocket and immediately it'll be missing. I have no clue how she loses things so quickly, but she's a master at it. It's like she's a one-way magician. She can disappear things wonderfully, but can never bring them back. I often have to find things for her. I don't mind all that much unless it's my stuff she loses. I have a rule that she can't use my things without asking. She's usually pretty good about following that rule.

We thank Tommy's mom once more as we start toward the door. Everyone continues out, I stay back to wait for Tommy. He says something to his mom. I don't know what. I'm not paying attention anyway. I've already begun thinking about the ride home.

Gotta stop back off at Charles' house to drop off the Ghostbuster gear and then gotta head home, which means we have to pass Stupid Dog's house again. Maybe I'll ask if I can keep the Proton Pack for today and give it back tomorrow. I'll Particle Accelerate the crap outta that dog! "Say hello to my little friend!" "Hasta la vista baby!"

Tommy is now standing in front of me. Has he been there long? I have no clue. Everyone is used to me checking out, so it's no big deal to them.

"Here," he smiles as he hands me the Batmobile. THE BATMOBILE! "It's the one from the back-up display," he explains.

I'm in shock. My mouth is open. My eyes are as wide as the tires on my bike as I take the coolest toy from my best friend's hand. "Thank you," I barely get it out. It's hushed and awkward.

"Come on!" he exclaims as he opens the door for me.

I follow him out, my gaze still on my treasure. He smiles at me and shakes his head. I shrug and put the toy in my pocket.

Everyone else is already mounted on their bikes and ready to ride, so Tommy and I mount our bikes. We're all still on the high of Cry Baby Road, and now I'm on an even higher high! I HAVE THE BATMOBILE! I come down, but only because I have to. One can't stay in the clouds for forever now can they? I take in a deep breath and look everyone over.

I pump my fist in the air, "Let's ride!"
Everyone follows suit, "LET'S RIDE!"

So we do. We ride. Not as usual, though. We take it slow this time. We're in no hurry to part ways. Today has been amazing and it's only half over! It's hard to imagine it getting any better than this! The scenic route usually stirs up conversations and story-telling since we've been all over this town, top to bottom. So the scenic route is perfect. This is our town. It belongs to us.

Usually, I'm the first one to blurt out the stories. Like the one time that all of us were climbing an apple tree we found growing out in a wooded area. While we were picking apples, all of a sudden the tree started falling! Split right in half under the weight of all of us! We were all screaming as it plummeted to the ground. It wasn't all that big of a tree, so none of us were hurt when we crash-landed. It sure makes for a fun story to tell, though! There was that one time we rode our bikes down a steep hill and I couldn't brake fast enough. I slammed right into a tree! It knocked me out cold! I woke up in the emergency room with a busted-up face and missing my top two front teeth! The things we walked away from... Good grief! We should have been injured way worse than we ever were. The stories are endless. Some of them make us laugh so hard when we think about them. Some of them could bring us to tears if we thought too much about them. One thing I'm glad for is the fact that, for the most part, we all share these stories together.

Well, I did it again. Spent the entire ride in my own world! We're at Charles' house. We ride into the yard, park our bikes, jump off and head inside. We shoot straight for Charles' room, no sign of his parents, probably getting ready for their company. We're shedding our Ghostbusters gear as we walk down the hallway to his room. Once inside, we lose the rest of the gear and pile it up on his bed.

"I'll get all this tomorrow if that's cool. There's no way I can ride all this back to my house on my bike." Jason looks at the pile of gear like it weighs a million pounds. I wouldn't be surprised if it did. I don't know. I've never tried to lift it all at once.

"Well okay." I look everyone over. "I guess we'll see you guys tomorrow!"

We all take turns high-fiving, then Matty and I head for the door. She grabs her Barbie comic as we exit Charles' bedroom. I can hear Tommy ask Charles if he can use the phone to call his Grandparents as we walk down the hallway to the stairs.

Outside, Matty and I pick up our bikes. She looks over at me and then down to her bike. "Let's walk 'em home. I'm tired."
"Sounds good," I agree.

I barely answer before Jason bursts out the door and sprints over to his bike. He smiles at us, does his best Elvis Presley shimmy, points at us, grabs his bike and races off. Oddly, the entire thing was one very fluid motion. He's been practicing.

Matty and I are creeping along. I guess the events tired everyone out a little. Today has been the longest half-day I think I've ever had.

"Think there's any French toast left?" Matty longingly asks. The look on her face says a lot.

"How in the world can you be hungry right now? We just ate lunch!"

Honestly, she's a bottomless pit when it comes to food! Mom says she's growing. I don't know. Matty shrugs it off. It seems like nothing ever bothers her. I wish I were more like that.

There's the stop sign, still bent. It still has yellow paint on it from the bus. I wonder if they'll ever fix it? It's been like... two years or something. I kind of hope they don't fix it. I hope it's always bent and always yellow on the edges. Maybe one day when I'm an old man I'll come back to this stop sign and tell my grandkids about Miss Sunshine, Jeremy Leaf, the Stop Sign and the Ditch. Sounds like a book title. I wonder if they'll laugh?

Hey! Look at that! I was right. We're walking our bikes. There's Stupid Dog and it's just sitting there, looking at us. It's almost like it's an actual dog and not a demon from the pits of the underworld sent here to terrify tiny insignificant children that once they cross its path have difficulties sleeping at night and

Bill and Felicia are done with their yard work. It looks good! Leaves raked, flower beds manicured.

"What you thinkin' about?" Matty asks.

"I don't know," I answer. "A lot, I guess. You ever notice that Stupid Dog never comes after us when we're just walking our bikes?"

"Yeah."

"What you mean, '*Yeah*'?"

"I've known that for a long time."

"No you haven't!" I'm shocked. I don't want to believe her, but Matty isn't a liar, so…

"Yes I have," she defends.

"Why haven't you ever said anything?"

"I like it when we get chased! It's fun," she admits through a smile.

"You are the craziest person in the entire world!"

Matty laughs at the thought, "Maybe!"

We finally make it onto our block. After the full day we've had in half the time, I'm very relieved to be almost home. Something looks different. A canary yellow car is parked outside the house.

"Who's here?" Matty asks.

The car is unfamiliar. Never seen this one before. And trust me, I would have remembered *this* car. Such a strange car. It's a car, with a friggin bed in the back like a pick-up truck. It's canary yellow and has two black racing stripes down the hood, roof and tailgate.

"I don't know," I answer.

We park our bikes and enter the house. There on the couch sits a man we've never seen before. A very firm man with a stone jaw and dark features. He smiles a large smile and rises to his feet. He's tall. He's big.

FOUR

"Oh hey, guys! I wasn't expecting you back so soon!" Mom chimes as she walks into the living room from the kitchen.

She hands the stranger a glass of sweet tea. The awkward silence is audible. Like that high-pitched ringing you can randomly hear sometimes.

Matty pipes up, "Who are you?"

Mom and whatever-his-name-is share a laugh at Matty's mandatory ice breaker.

"My name is Chris. Your mom has told me so much about the two of you."
"Like what?" Matty asks.

They laugh again.

With a big smile, Chris says, "Like how straightforward you are and how you, sir," looking at me now with his brown, almost black eyes, "you're a dreamer," he finishes. Mom smiles at that last part.

A dreamer? What's that supposed to mean? I don't mind if Mom says stuff like that, but who the heck is this guy? Why am I so irritated with him? He hasn't done anything wrong, other than not thanking Mom for the sweet tea. I can let that slide for now though. This little introduction is not comfortable for anyone. It's easy to forget manners, I guess.

He honestly seems nice, but he's not like Mom's other friends. All of them are our friends too. If this guy is so great, how come she's never told us about him? I've never heard his name before now. This is weird. We should have stayed out longer. Maybe we should go back out? Wait a second! Is that why there was so much French toast this morning?! How long has Chris been here?!

Clearly, every thought I'm thinking is showing on my face as Mom jumps in to direct the conversation to a less awkward topic.

"So we were thinking that maybe we could all go out for pizza and a movie tonight! Maybe get to know each other a little?"

Dang.   Pizza AND A MOVIE? She got me. She knows me all too well. My Kryptonite. Pizza AND a movie. Fine. I can endure Chris for pizza and a movie.

What's my problem?   Why am I so against this guy? Take a chill pill dude! Give him a chance!

I do what seems like the right thing and step up to shake his hand. Why? I don't know. I still haven't said a word, and honestly, I'm looking for a way out here.

Man, this is awkward.

Chris looks at Mom and then back to me. He takes my hand and shakes it. I don't know what to say, so I turn around and head to my room. Matty follows me inside and I close the door behind us.

"I wonder what movie we're going to see," Matty says.

"I don't know," I reply as I hand over her Catwoman toy from my pocket. I bring out my Batman and Batmobile as I take a seat at the edge of my bed. Matty immediately starts to play with her new toy, jumping from imaginary rooftop to imaginary rooftop, I assume.   For once in my life I'm not in the playing mood. I don't know why the awkward exchange in the living room has set me off, but it has. Matty notices and requires an answer.

"Why aren't you playing? What's wrong?"
"I think Chris is Mom's boyfriend," I admit. And that's it. It dawns on me as it shoots out of my mouth. That's what is upsetting me.
"Gross," Matty responds.
"I'm serious."
"It's still gross."

Matty stares at me as I stare at my Batmobile. I don't have anything. I mean, I can feel something churning deep down... but I haven't put my finger on it just yet. There is something.   I'm just not aware of what *it* is exactly. Not yet.

"So what then?   Mom seems to like him," Matty offers.
"Just forget it," I give up.

I tuck my Batman and Batmobile under my pillow as I lay down and pull out the comic I have hidden. I begin to flip through the pages mindlessly. As I lay on my back, staring at the words and images, I find my mind drifting back to Mom and Chris. I'm looking at the pictures, but I'm not *seeing* the pictures. I can't focus.

Mom has a lot of guy friends, so it's not the fact that Chris is a guy that bothers me. All of Mom's

The next thing I know, I'm waking up. Well, Matty is waking me up.

"Get up! We're leaving in a couple of minutes."

"What? How long have I been asleep?" I ask sleepily. I'm trying to regain consciousness.

"I dunno. It's 4 o'clock though."

"4 o'clock?" There's the motivation I need. I'm awake. "Why'd you let me sleep so long?"

"You didn't tell me to wake you up! How was I supposed to know you were going to hibernate?" she calls as she leaves the room.

I throw my legs off the side of my bed, dead weight. My body is still deep in the sleep zone. You know, that hard sleep where you drool all over your pillow. There's no dreaming in that zone. You're too far gone. I had no clue I'd even fallen asleep, much less crashed for three-plus hours!

I wonder if Batman sleeps this hard after he saves Gotham City? Okay… let's do this.

I barely make it out of bed before Mom opens the door to my bedroom.

"Knock, knock, sleepyhead! You've been out cold!"

"Yeah, I didn't mean to fall asleep," I respond slowly.

"Must've needed it. Go ahead and get cleaned up. We're out the door in five, okay?"

"Yes ma'am."

Mom shoots me a smile and leaves. Groggy, I make my way to the bathroom, flick the light switch on and immediately see that a hat is going to be mandatory for this evening's festivities.

Geez. How did Mom keep a straight face just now?

By the looks of it, standing under Niagara Falls is the only thing that can fix this hair. Spiky hair is cool and all, but this spiky (what I'm currently dealing with)? Not so much! I brush my teeth and splash cold water over my face. Afterward, I step back into my room and grab my Orlando Magic ball cap that I always leave hanging on the bedpost, throw it on backward and step into the living room.

I'm immediately met by everyone's gaze: Matty, Mom, Chris.

Oh yeah. Chris. Okay.

"Sorry," I muster. "Didn't know you all were waiting on me."

Matty starts in, "I told you-"

"Not at all!" She's cut off by Chris. "But since you're here and ready, let's jet!"

We step out into the crisp fall evening. The air refreshes me and helps me to wake up fully.

"I'd say let's take the El Camino, but there isn't enough room for all of us," Chris informs.

"We can take our car," Mom responds.

Mom tosses the keys to Chris as she steps to the passenger seat. He's not going to open the door for her? First no manners with the sweet tea and now no manners here? I sit behind Mom and Matty behind Chris. As soon as Chris sits he starts the car and pulls a cassette tape from his jean jacket pocket all in one go.

***Why? Why is this man just
carrying around a tape in his pocket?***

"Salt-N-Peppa," he declares as he holds the tape up for all to see. After a long moment, much too long, he slides the tape into the tape deck and presses play. With a cheesy bob of his head, he puts the car into drive and pulls out onto the road. He's clearly into this. It's all right. I prefer rock-n-roll, but that's just what Mom has raised us on. I'm open to new things, I guess. After a few minutes on the road, Chris pulls into Pizza Hut. Score! Pizza Hut is my favorite! Things are looking up. We all climb out and make our way into the restaurant.

We take a seat in a booth with Mom and Chris on one side, Matty and me on the other. The waitress walks up to our table. She's a high school girl, for sure. And she's cute. *Extremely* cute. I can't let Matty catch wind of the fact that I think so. She'll completely and utterly embarrass me. She'll say how she's trying to help, but she's just so aggressive that it'll blow any chance I have. Or could ever *dream* of having. Forget the fact that I'm only 12 and she's probably 17.

Chris orders one large pepperoni and one large veggie lovers. I don't plan on getting anywhere near that veggie lovers. I'm a pepperoni man through and through.

The Aphrodite of waitresses takes our order and leaves. Matty immediately turns to me and whispers.

"You like her?"
"No," I'm quick with my answer. I have to be. It's life or death.
"I'll talk to her for you."
"Don't. Please!" I beg.

She smiles. I know Matty means well. She just wants to help. Mom takes notice of the hushed commotion coming from our side of the table.

"What are you two whispering about over there?" She's all smiles. She knows.
"Nothing!" Again, I'm quick to answer.

Please, God!   Let someone or something change the topic!

"What did you guys end up doing today?" Mom asks, coming through with the perfect question to distract from my blushing face.

Oh, thank you, God!   Mom for the win!

Matty jumps right in with all the details and enthusiasm of our day, leaving out very little.

"Bill and Felicia were raking their yard early this morning."

"You don't say?" Mom is so sweet. She seems to genuinely care about everything we say. She's never given us a reason to believe that she doesn't care.

"Yeah, there were like four million bags of leaves!" Matty continues.

Mom feigns surprise, "Four million, you say?" She looks to me for confirmation. I subtly shake my head. There were eight. Eight total. And that was when they were completely finished.

"Yep!" Matty confirms. "And then Stupid Dog nearly got us this time, Mom!"

"Stupid Dog?" Chris asks.

Matty just keeps plowing ahead with the story. "After Stupid Dog, we passed the Sunshine Stop Sign and then Charles' house, where I ate a chocolate-covered doughnut with sprinkles on it!"

Mom tries to stop the conversation there, but Matty has too much momentum behind her. Even if Mom were able to get a word in, Matty is motor-mouthing, so she's not stopping until the story is over. I wish Mom would interject.

Please interject just long enough to miss Cry Baby Road...

"And then we rode all the way down Cry Baby Road! And guess what!"

There it is. Mom's eyes go wide. "You did what now?"

I sink back into the booth. If I could sink through it, I would.

"We rode down Cry Baby Road," Matty repeats proudly.

Mom looks at me, the supposed voice of reason. Chris leans forward in his seat with a flare of interest and a crooked grin growing across his face.

"You must be something special. I've heard nobody rides it and comes out alive," his grin growing wider.

My chest puffs up, and for the first time, I'm excited to talk to Chris. For some reason, I burst out.

"We rode it ALL THE WAY THROUGH! Didn't stop until we hit the intersection on the other side!"

Mom shoots Chris a playful look of disappointment, "Don't encourage them!"

Chris' response is slick, "What? Kids'll be kids, right?"

"I know that's right!" Matty chimes in, and we all laugh.

At the movies, Chris loads us up with popcorn, candy and pop, against Mom's paper-thin demands. That's pretty cool of him.

Called it.   Dang.   Chris is holding Mom's hand.   Weird.   What does this mean?   Mom hasn't been with anyone since Dad.

Dad.   Man, I haven't thought of him in a while.   I wonder what he would say.   Well, I've only seen him a couple of times since he left, so… Eh.   Who cares what Dad would say? Apparently, I do.   I guess Mom having Chris means that Dad really won't be coming back.   Maybe that's why I treated Chris so weird at first.

Well, this sucks.   Totally ruining the movie. Just forget it. Just watch the movie.

On the ride home from the movies, I turn my attention to the night sky.   I love the stars.   I love outer space.   Staring into it is just so calming.   It's a seemingly scattered mess that's also organized.   Like me.

We pull up to the house and park.   Matty has dozed off so I tap her on the shoulder, "Hey, we're home."

She mumbles something about a bear and starts shuffling towards the door as I start to get out.   I help guide my zombie of a sister through the front door.   As I lead Matty to our room, I call out, "Night guys!"

"Goodnight!" Mom and Chris respond in unison.

I lead Matty to her bed and take her shoes off as she slams face-first into her pillow, already fast asleep. I throw a blanket over her and walk to my bed. As I sit and recall the day, I find myself holding on to all the fun stuff and trying to forget the feeling I had in the movie theater. Which is kind of hard to do when I can still hear Chris' voice in the living room.

> *I need to remember the excitement of being with my friends and the Cry Baby Road victory, and... OH YEAH!*

I reach under my pillow and pull out my Batman and Batmobile. I kick off my shoes and lay back. I flip the light switch off on my way down and let the moonlight from my window light the edges and curves of the Batmobile. I examine it in the dark and imagine it on the streets of Gotham City. I imagine driving it. I imagine *I'm* Batman, driving *my* Batmobile down Cry Baby Road and I drift off to sleep.

The next morning I'm up before Matty. She's still fast asleep and has hair... in her mouth. She's sleeping hard, I guess. I must have slept pretty hard myself. First off, I never removed my Orlando Magic ball cap. I slept in it and it somehow stayed on all night! Second, I had some crazy vivid dreams. I mean, I know I did, but I can't remember any of them. I remember flashes of things, but nothing solid. They all crammed into each other to make one really weird, really long dream.

It's Sunday. Toon day! We're all going to meet up at Tommy's house and watch the latest episodes of the shows we love most. I'd better get moving! I shuffle out of the room and into the living room. It's quiet. I'm even up before Mom. That's odd. Mom is usually up before us both. I go to the kitchen and pour myself a bowl of cereal. I take a seat at the table and listen to myself crunch the crap out of some Fruity Pebbles. It's dumb how loud you are when you're trying to be quiet.

The quiet is a strange place. You hear noises you wouldn't normally hear, like the weird hum the refrigerator makes and that creek the dining room chair makes when you lean from one side to the other. I hear a toilet flush and Mom talking. She rounds the corner, as does Chris.

Wait. CHRIS?! What the crap?!

FIVE

My face must be saying *exactly* what I'm thinking. Maybe something along the lines of, "WHAT THE CRAP?!" because Mom and Chris look at each other, to me, then back to one another. Finally, Mom attempts some sort of weak response.

"Oh, hey! I um…" Mom's stumped. I'm stumped. Chris seems fine. Why is Chris so fine? Why is Chris here? What is happening?

Chris quickly deflects, "Mornin'! Whatcha eatin'?" His smooth talk might work on Mom, but not on me.
"Cereal," I reply bluntly. I don't tell him what kind, he has eyes. I hope he gets the message. I take a bite of cereal to somehow show I mean business.

> *Dang it. Top part is good, bottom part is soggy. Dang Chris and his timing. Ruining all sorts of crap.*

Mom looks at Chris, "Could you give us a couple of minutes?"

Chris replies with a nod and then disappears back through the living room. She turns her attention to me and slowly walks to the kitchen table. She doesn't sit. She grips the back of the chair in front of her and looks at me.

"I know you probably have questions," she begins. I quickly shovel a bite of cereal into my mouth. Look, Fruity Pebbles are awesome and all, but once those suckers get soggy there's not quite as much awesomeness in each spoonful.

"I know you just met Chris, but I've been seeing him for quite some time now and last night-"
"Okay," I interrupt. I don't want to hear anything else. I don't want to talk about any kind of topic that this could lead to. I didn't ask for all of this. However, I don't want to hurt my Mom.

I just woke up. I just want to eat my Fruity Pebbles. I just want to go to Tommy's house.

Mom pulls out the chair and takes a seat. She leans in close to me, eye to eye.

"Okay what?" she asks. She's wanting to talk this out.
"Okay Chris, I guess," I say with a weak shrug. It's all I can muster. I'm trying.
"Give him a chance. I really do think you're going to like him a lot."

"Okay," I reply. A moment passes as Mom looks into my eyes.

"Okay."

We sit in silence for a minute. It feels more like a year. I take another bite of cereal.

Great. All soggy now. What a morning. I'm still hungry though and at this point, I'm not sure what I'll say if Mom starts up another conversation. I'll just keep shoveling Soggy Pebbles into my mouth.

"You guys going to Tommy's today?" Mom asks, trying to make things a little less awkward.

Now, this is a subject I can handle!

"Yeah, we have to see what's up with this Green Ranger dude!" I respond excitedly. Mom smiles. She's happy I'm talking and acting more like myself again, I suppose.

"But for real, the Green Ranger came out of nowhere and he's got everything all jacked up!" I continue.

She smiles. I smile. I do hope Mom is happy. I want her to be, and that's why I'm going to attempt her request. I'm going to 'give Chris a chance.'

Mom rises from her seat. "Tonight it'll just be us three. We'll do something fun, okay?"
"Okay," I concede.

She pats the chair like there's more she wants to say, or maybe she wants me to say something more, but neither of us do.

"I love you," she says with a smile.
"Love you too, Mom."

With that, she turns and leaves. I immediately stand and dump the rest of my Soupy Pebbles into the garbage disposal in the sink. I grab a package of Pop-Tarts for myself and one for Matty, then head to the bedroom.

> *I've gotta wake her up. We've gotta get out of here. Mom and Chris are in her room.   I'm not stupid. I'm 12.*

I open the door to the bedroom, which wakes Matty. I toss the Pop-Tarts on my bed and head to the closet. I grab something for myself: a white T with neon patterns and a pair of jeans.

"What do you wanna wear?" I call from the closet.

"What time is it?" Matty asks sleepily.

"Dunno. It's time to go to Tommy's though!"

"I want my pink shirt and my white pants."

I grab both and toss them to her as I walk out of the closet. I'm in a hurry. Matty sits up and stretches. I quickly lose my PJs and jump into my jeans and T-shirt.

"Come on," I say over my shoulder as I make my bed. "Let's go."

"Why are you rushing me?" She asks, annoyed.

"The guys are waiting on us."

"The guys are always waiting on us!"

I don't want Matty to see Chris here. I don't want her to ask questions. She won't ask Mom, she'll ask me. I don't want to have to answer those questions. I need a distraction. I don't know what. I bend over and pick up the Pop-Tarts, and like an answer to prayer, there it is. One of the packages of Pop-Tarts is blueberry and the other is chocolate. Matty will fist-fight for chocolate. I turn with the new-found opportunity and address her. I hold up both packages.

"If you don't hurry up, I'll eat the last package of chocolate and you'll have to eat the blueberry," I finish with a mischievous grin.

"You better not!"

"I'll do it and I'll loooooove it!"

Matty springs into action. PJs off, clothes on, bed made, she even manages to brush her hair - her slobber hair

- and have it back in a ponytail in record time! She moves like the Flash, or Quicksilver, or whatever super-powered speedster you prefer.

"I'm ready," she finalizes as she lunges for the packaged chocolate breakfast pastries.

"I'm going to threaten your chocolate more often," I reply in awe. I literally have never seen her move that fast. Incredible.

We make our way out of the room and pass Mom's room. Quiet. Okay. At least Matty isn't going to see Chris. We open the front door and the first thing out of Matty's mouth as we step on the porch is, "Chris is still here?"

The figgin' El Camino!
Dang it!
I didn't think about her seeing Chris' car!

We kick back the kickstands and walk our bikes. We know each other well enough to know what the other is thinking from time to time. In this very moment, we're both thinking, "Not today Stupid Dog." We steer our bikes with one hand and eat our breakfast with the other.

"Did Chris come over early this morning too?"
"No," I say, hoping that will curb her curiosity. It doesn't.

"His car is still at the house."

"He stayed the night."

"Why?" Matty persists.

"I don't know, Sis."

"I don't understand."

"It's okay. I don't really either."

We walk on, by Bill and Felicia's house, past Stupid Dog's house and his stupid little beady eyes. We pass the Sunshine Stop Sign and there, out of danger's jaws, we stop. We have to ride the rest of the way or it would take us all day to get to Tommy's house. It's a quiet ride, which is unusual for Matty. We both have a lot to think about.

> *Come to think of it, I wonder how it's affecting her. She's never known Mom to be with a man at all! Dad left when she was a baby. It's only been us three her whole life. She's 10! Wow. Maybe I should try and talk to her about it?*

We get to Tommy's house after an extended ride through town. It looks like Charles is the only other one of us here. I don't see Jason's bike. His parents could have given him a ride. Maybe he's not here yet. We park our bikes and walk up to Tommy's house. His Grandpa opens the door. Tommy and his Mom live with his Grandparents, or maybe his Grandparents live with them. Seems like the exact same thing to me. Who cares? His Grandpa is really nice but is hard of hearing, so everything is a tad loud around him.

"HI-YA THERE KIDS! COME ON IN!"

"THANKS!" we reply. We're trying not to scream, yet still trying to be loud enough for him to hear us. Fine line. Very fine line.

He closes the door behind us as we enter.

"TOMMY'S IN THE BACKROOM!   GO ON BACK!"

We make our way to the "backroom". It's just another living room in the house, but it's filled with all of Tommy's toys and playthings. Tommy is turning on the TV and Charles is seated, cross-legged on the floor in anticipation. Tommy looks back at us as we enter.

"Hey guys! Just in time! Come sit down!" We quickly trot over to sit next to Charles.

"Sup guys!" He gives us high-fives as we plop down.

"Where's Jason?" I ask.

Tommy pushes in the VHS tape and backs up to make sure it's working.

"Oh, he was too late getting home yesterday, so his Dad is making him do chores today," Tommy explains as he studies the TV screen. Snowy static.

I begin to respond, "That sucks, I wonder if -," but Tommy quickly interrupts my train of thought.

"HEY GRANDPA!   IS THIS THING ON THE RIGHT CHANNEL OR-"

The screen flickers to life and the TV announcer's voice barrels through, "Previously on The Mighty Morphin' Power Rangers!"

"NEVERMIND!" Tommy belts over his shoulder.

Tommy's Grandpa, late to the party, "WHAT? WHAT'S THAT TOMMY?"

"NOTHIN! IT'S OKAY!" Tommy shouts.

Of course, Tommy's Grandpa enters the room anyway. "WHAT'S THAT YOU SAY THERE, TOMMY?"

> *We're on a ticking time clock here! We're about to pick up where we left off!*
> ***THE GREEN RANGER!!!***

Charles, Matty and I are all talking over each other, telling Tommy to pause the VCR so we don't miss anything. Tommy, who still hasn't taken a seat, is trying to deal with us, his screaming Grandfather and the TV all at the same time.   All this while panicking because the episode is seconds away from starting. He's baffled.

"I, uh…" He turns to the VCR.

"TOMMY, I HEARD YOU CALL ME. EVERYTHING OKAY?" Tommy's Grandpa asks.

"YEAH!   I JUST-," Tommy shouts while simultaneously trying to acknowledge his Grandpa and look for the pause button.

"Pause it! Pause the tape!" Matty and I chant. We both understand that it's not really helping the situation, but it's all we can think to do. Of course, no one else rushes to Tommy's aide. We're all sort of frozen in this very loud panicked moment.

"YOU KIDS NEED A LITTLE HELP WITH THE VCR? IT CAN BE TRICKY!" Grandpa offers.

Tommy's head is spinning. Not literally, obviously. That would be crazy to see, but it must be close. This is one of the funniest things to see. He's flustered and can't handle it. He keeps turning back and forth between VCR and Grandpa. Grandpa is closing in and Tommy keeps pushing the Pause/Play button over and over again because he thinks it didn't work. What's actually happening is he's unpausing, thinking he paused it, but it's playing. Therefore he tries to pause it and he's confused himself into a terrible cycle of pause/un-pause! I can't hold it any longer. I burst out laughing. I can't contain it!

Everyone turns and looks at me. The tape is finally paused, and so is Grandpa. Tommy has this look on his face, with actual sweat, that makes me laugh even harder. Matty starts cracking up with me. If one of us loses it, the other is shortly behind. We can't help it. After a few more seconds Charles joins in, then Tommy. Grandpa gives up.

"YOU KIDS! YOU'RE PLAYIN TRICKS ON ME! SHAME, SHAME!" Grandpa playfully accuses.

His response, and lack of understanding in the situation, hits me even harder and I nearly lose my breath in laughter. We're all doubled over now. Grandpa chuckles to himself and shuffles out of the room. After about five minutes we collect ourselves and Tommy pushes play. He has to immediately pause it again because the fact that he actually found the play button makes me crack up all over again. I guess I needed to laugh. I guess we all did.

It was a good morning. We watched our Toons and said our goodbyes. Riding along, Matty starts singing and we make it home without incident. No Stupid Dog. It must've been inside. Good. And look at that! No El Camino! Chris is gone. Tonight will be good. Just us.

Six

The next couple of weeks blow by super fast. School is… school. Pizza, bikes, comics, video games and cartoons, The Crew! Chris comes around our house a lot more, and as promised, I've been giving him "a chance". It's getting easier.

A couple of weeks ago he took us to the mall that's in the next town over, just Him, Matty and myself. I was hesitant at first but went along with it. He promised we could stop at the toy store there. That toy store has toys we can't find anywhere else! Of course I had to go! I wore a bandana under my Orlando Magic ball cap, on backward - naturally. I saw Axel Rose do it from Guns N' Roses, so I felt the need to do the same. Anyway, the mall cop stopped us as soon as we walked through the doors and told me I had to take my bandana off. He said something about, "gangs are getting bad." I dunno. Chris responded with, "The kid is 11." The mall cop wouldn't back down. He kept insisting I remove my bandana. I didn't see the big deal, so I removed my ball cap and went for the bandana. Chris put his hand on my arm to stop me. I remember it felt heavy and hot. I wanted to pull away but honestly didn't know what to do. This was getting tense. Chris stepped in closer to the officer, and even though he was looking him dead in the eye, he spoke to me. "You can keep your bandana on. You're just a kid." Then, without breaking his gaze, he switched the conversation back to him and the cop. "Ain't that right officer?" After what seemed like an eternity, the officer nodded. Chris turned to us and winked as the officer turned. I felt bad for the mall cop. He was just doing his job. I also felt bad about feeling good about being able to keep my bandana on.

This is it. This is the greatest holiday that has ever been, other than Christmas… and my birthday. I know that my birthday isn't globally celebrated, but it should be. Back to the most thrilling night of the year, Halloween! I go as a werewolf, Matty is the Pink Ranger, Tommy goes as someone from Star Trek. Tommy is a Trekky. I don't understand why. I mean, everyone is allowed to love what they love and all, but there is Star Wars.

Anyway! Tommy is someone from Star Trek. I don't know who. He's told me a few times, but it escapes me every time. He has the perfect opportunity to go as the Green Ranger! Both of their names are Tommy! I can't wrap my brain around it. Charles is a ninja, a dead one. Charles always wants to go as a dead something. One year he was a dead football player, one year a dead doctor. I dunno. And then for like the tenth year in a row, Jason is Elvis. He's been the 50's Elvis, the Blue Suede Shoes Elvis, The Rhinestone Elvis, The Jailhouse Rock Elvis. This year he took cues from Charles and he's going as dead

Elvis. He very well could be the Red Ranger, same name, but he's sticking with Elvis.

"Dude. You've got to stop with Elvis!" I try and reason with him.

His response every time, "Hey mamma! Don't step on my Blue Suede Shoes!"

November comes. November is usually a lot of fun. We normally see family around Thanksgiving and Matty's birthday is toward the end of the month! Plus how could anyone forget that Christmas is literally right around the corner? The anticipation build-up is crazy! Chris is staying at the house a lot more, and because of that we're seeing less and less of Mom's friends. I'm not a fan of that part. However, one perk of Chris staying over more and more is he rents a lot of movies for Matty and me to watch! He also runs two VCRs at the same time, one to play the movie and the other to record it onto a blank VHS tape. So we pretty much get to keep every movie we ever watch! I'll give him points for that.

Chris likes beer. A lot. Beer's never been in the house before, but Chris keeps the fridge stocked. For Thanksgiving Chris talks Mom into going to his family's house instead of Grandma and Grandpa's house like always. I don't like it, but I keep quiet about it. Things are different, but I keep quiet. I told Mom I'd "give Chris a chance". It's not like I really have a say anyway, right?

We meet Chris' Mom and his brother Ben. They seem nice. His Dad lives in a different state. Chris says we'll meet him later. We have Thanksgiving dinner with them. It's not as good as Grandma's. Maybe I'm being a turd. Maybe I'm pouting. I need to "give them a chance". Chris' Mom seems nice, but she smells like onions. Hopefully, that's because she's been cooking. There's always a chance though, a chance that she's just a stinky woman. Ben seems like a fun guy. He acts crazy and is funny.

Okay. Enough of all that. It's T-minus 5 days until Matty's birthday! Mom pulled me aside a couple of days ago to start planning the party. Matty's so excited! Her favorite color is pink. At least for now. The Pink Ranger, if she ever changed colors I think Matty's favorite color would change right along with her. So naturally, Matty's party will be decked out in pink.

It's go time. Mom gives me a mission. I have to get Matty to talk. If she could only get one thing for her birthday, what would it be? We have to be as minimal as "one" because if we said any number more she'd never decide. The list would never stop. Of course, she'll get more than one present from family, friends and party goers, but Mom always wants to get us that one present that just blows us away. The one thing that makes us forget about all the other presents. The one thing that she can use as leverage in grounding if we're not being the kids we're raised to be.

I walk in the room. Matty is sprawled across her bed on her stomach, coloring. She's kicking her feet back and forth, humming the song she made up.

"Whatcha coloring?" I try to act nonchalant.

"A dog." She lifts the page up so I can see it. "A pink dog."

"I don't believe I've ever seen a pink dog before."

She turns and smiles, "That's why I'm coloring this one pink."

I take a seat on my bed, thinking of how I can start up the conversation that will get Mom her answers, all while not alerting Matty that we're up to something.

"I'm definitely asking for the Batmobile for Christmas," I try.

"I know! You've told me like a million times!" She belts, obviously irritated at my announcement. In her defense, I have said it quite a bit, and often. I can't help it. The small one that Tommy gave me is awesome, but to have that big one. Oh, man!

"Yeah. I just can't stop thinking about it!"

Matty doesn't respond. Coloring is way more important than my obsession.

"You haven't said what you want." I'm fishing now.

Matty stops coloring and looks up, "I've been thinking." She pops up to sitting. This is it! I'll get the intel that Mom desires and be on my way.

"But there's just so much that I want," she continues.

Dang. Should've known it wouldn't be that easy. I need to prod her along.

"Well, you do have your birthday in a few days, and then Christmas," I'm giving it all I've got here. "You have time to decide for Christmas. What you gonna ask for your birthday? If you could only pick one thing?"

"That's easy!   I want the Pink Ranger toy!" Boom! I should slowly make my way to the living room to inform Mom. Slowly so I don't alert Matty. Slowly.

"And I want the Yellow Ranger!   And the Command Center! And I need bad guys for them to fight! And I want…" And there she goes. My head drops a little. The floodgates are open. Mom asked for the one major thing and my sister is unloading her mental catalog of "Number Ones".

"But which one? If you could only pick ONE?" I interject.
"Oh, ummmmmmmm, I guess it would have to be-."

She's deep in thought. Good. She can only pick one.

"The Pink Ranger," She decides.   She seems unsure. She is squinting like she's trying to read something a mile away. I wait. She finally arrives, "Yep!" She's finally made her mind up. Fairly painless too! Okay.

I need to make my way to Mom now. I get up and "examine" something on our bookshelf as a disguise of why I'm standing. I need to linger but not so long that she asks me what I'm doing. A secret agent can't get caught! I act as if I forgot something and make my way to the door.

"Tell Mom everything I said. Not just the Pink Ranger," she calls with a smile as I exit. Dang it! Busted. I was doing so well! The subtle questions, the book-shelf, the remembering something outside the room, not good enough. Next time I have to do better.

The party is a hit! Matty wasn't expecting such a big party! I was able to at least keep that part a secret. Chris pitched in with Mom and they got Matty the Pink and Yellow Ranger, a couple of Puttys and they even got her the Command Center! Geez!

Mom acts surprised when my sister opens her presents. Mom's so cool. Matty is having fun, we all are. All the guys are here, and Ben, Chris' brother is here. I wasn't expecting him honestly, so that's cool of him to come. A couple of Matty's girlfriends from school are here. It's a big party!

I'm pretty stoked about the cake. I talked Matty into getting an ice cream cake. Those are my favorite, and since my birthday isn't until the Summer, I may have just suggested it very heavily on more than one occasion. She agreed and didn't really care much as long as it was chocolate. It's not just chocolate, though. It's chocolate ice cream with chocolate cake. It's the greatest invention since Snickers Ice Cream bars.

The party comes to a close and Matty says goodbye to her friends. The guys all say goodbye and give out the high fives and everyone starts going their own way. Ben stays behind and is hanging out with Chris, drinking beer. Now that I think about it, none of Mom's friends came. That's odd because they're all so close. I wonder why.

"Will you help me set up the Command Center?" Matty asks me, grinning from ear to ear. She knows good and well that we're going to be staying up way too late playing with that thing! I agree. No arm-twist needed! I'm just as excited as she is! I grab the massive box, Mom and Matty each grab an arm full of birthday loot and we all make our way back to our bedroom.

Ben calls out to Matty on our way back, "Happy birthday little woman!"

"Thanks, Ben!"

We don't stop for pleasantries. There's no time. Time is of the essence. The Command Center is calling! Mom drops the gear, tells us she loves us and takes her leave. Matty and I spend the next three hours setting up and playing with her new Power Ranger toys.

The next thing we know we're startled by Mom's screams. We rush out of our room to see Chris and Ben in a fistfight! What the crap?! Brothers aren't supposed to fight! Mom is screaming, "STOP IT! STOP IT!"

They don't stop. They are wailing on each other. I step in front of Matty and make myself as big as I can in our doorway. She settles in behind me. I can't believe what I'm seeing! Chris gets Ben in a headlock and they topple over and onto the coffee table, smashing it to pieces. Mom grabs a pillow from the couch and throws it at both of them.

"STOP IT NOW!"

She screams loud. Very loud. They stop. There's a hush as both Chris and Ben lay on the floor, side by side, panting for their breath. Mom turns and sees Matty and me staring.
"No! No! No!" She runs to us and nudges us back into our bedroom. "What did you see?"

It's out before I can even think, "Chris and Ben kicking the crap out of each other! What's going on Mom?!"

A tear slides down Mom's face. With that tear, Matty starts crying. I'm in shock. Mom steps up to us and throws her arms around us. "It's going to be okay kiddos. Momma's gonna fix it."

> *Fix what? The table? The fight? How do you fix a fight? The fact that we'd never even seen two men fight in real life, but now it was literally right in front of us in our living room? Power Rangers and X-Men and Batman is one thing, but real people, drinking real beer, being real drunk, getting into a real fistfight, that's different.*

We've never even been around beer or drunk people. It was movie stuff. Not real. Now all of a sudden, on Matty's birthday, in our house it's all very real.

SEVEN

December is here. Chris is living with us now. He smooth-talked his way out of the "incident". Ben doesn't really come over anymore. I think Chris blamed him for what happened. I'm not so sure that's the case. I'm not really sure what he could have said for her to agree to him living with us, but it must have been good.

It's too cold to ride bikes to school now, so Mom drops us off. We've started riding the bus again, but only after school. We have a different bus driver now. No more Miss Sunshine. Charles is on the same route as us, so that makes for some fun rides. At 3:00 pm, the bell rings and all the kids burst out of their classrooms and fill the hallways. I make my way to the bus line.

"Hey wait up!" I hear Charles behind me.

I turn and address him with a smile and nod. He comes trotting up and alongside me.

"You got homework?" he asks.
"Yeah, a little," I admit.
"Man, I hate homework."
"You know anyone that loves homework?" I ask sarcastically.

He immediately responds with, "I bet Emily loves homework." His grin looks like the Cheshire Cat's. It's like he was hoping the conversation would open up to this, and I walked right into it. My face is hot. Emily is the smartest kid in our class, I also just so happen to have the littlest, teeny tiniest, crush on her. My dumb butt told Charles for some reason, and now he mentions it every dang minute he can.

"Shut up Chuck!" I bark, flushed.
"Hey man! I'm just sayin!" His grin doesn't fade.

Matty comes bounding up. Perfect timing!

"I drew a picture of a Unicorn pooping on the back of my math sheet today!"
"Classy," I respond with a chuckle.
"How'd Mrs. Butler like that?" asked Charles.
Matty turns to us, sidestepping as she walks, and responds with her best sinister whisper, "She doesn't know yet."

We all share a laugh as we exit the school corridor to board our bus. Bus number 27. All manner of crazies ride number 27. Leaf and his goons are still on board, so the level of loud is that of a continual Tyrannosaurus roar. Madness. Charles, Matty and I have learned that the sound is considerably low behind Leaf's row, so that's where we sit. Every once in a while he'll turn around and try and carry on some kind of conversation with us. It never sticks, which is more than fine with me.

The bus stops at our house so Matty and I exit. Odd, Chris' car is here. He should still be at work. Mom's not here, just Chris. We enter and Chris is sprawled out, asleep on the couch. There are several beer cans on the floor.

"Come on Sis. Let's go to our room."
"I'm hungry," Matty challenges.

She heads for the kitchen. I follow, hesitantly, my eyes never leaving the drunken bear. In the kitchen, Matty climbs the countertop and starts digging around for some junk food.

"Are all the Pop-Tarts gone?"
"Yes. Keep your voice down," I chide.

Her head is all the way in the cupboard now.

"WHAT?" She asks, a little too loud.
"I SAID," I quickly look back toward the living room. Still sleeping. I continue, a little more hushed now, "I said keep your voice down."

Matty hops down from the counter with a thud. I watch with extreme anxiety as the door to the cupboard slams shut on its own. I flinch with the slam. As I open my eyes I notice Matty staring at something behind and above me. I turn and immediately notice Chris standing there. I can smell the beer on his breath. His eyes are red. Dang it. We woke the beer bear.

"Didn't notice I was tryin' to sleep in there?" His words are slurred.

"Sorry," Matty replies sheepishly. "I didn't mean to."

I turn and take a step back, "It was an accident." My tone is much braver than intended. Chris huffs and takes a drink of beer. The man's a magician. NOW he doesn't have a beer, NOW he does!

I just want to go, but we can't.

> *He's blocking the only way out of the kitchen, more like clogging it. I guess we could go out the back door to the backyard? This is stupid. What then? Are we just going to stand here? Matty with a friggin' snack cake in her hand, me with a stupid look on my face and Chris chugging a bottomless can of beer?*

Chris takes another drink of beer. Empty. He shakes the can and then turns his attention to it.

"If your Mom asks for me I went to get more beer," He says as he turns and leaves.

A massive wave of oxygen hits me. I must have been holding my breath.

Matty quickly shoots past me and I follow. I close the bedroom door behind me and lock it. I need to make sure we're protected... somehow.

"I know where we can be safe," I say as confidently as I can.
"Where?" Matty asks.
"Get your homework and crawl under my bed."
"What?" Matty asks, confused.
"Just trust me! It's like the Fortress of Solitude!"

That was a good enough answer for her, I guess. Matty grabs her backpack and crawls under my bed. I army crawl under the bed after her. I move some comics and a flashlight out of the way that I have hidden for "lights out time."

"We can hang out in here until Mom gets home."
"Okay."

Matty seems to take comfort. She's against the wall and I'm on the other side of her, making her what would be the white filling in an Oreo cookie. I guess that makes me one of the chocolate cookies. Could be worse I guess.

We work on our homework by the light of my "lights out" flashlight. I pull a pillow and blanket up along my side to shield me from whatever may come. For some reason that brings some comfort. Cool. We have our very own Fortress of Solitude.

Some time passes.   I don't know how much. Both of us are finished with our homework and I've started reading comics aloud to Matty.   A knock on the door interrupts us. The handle jiggles. Both Matty and I stare at each other, dead silent.

"Guys?" Mom's voice comes through the door.

Oh, thank goodness!

I quickly shimmy my way out from under the Fortress of Solitude and unlock the door. I can't help it, I attack Mom with a hug.

"Oh man!" she exclaims. I guess I did spring it on her without warning. I couldn't help it! She peels me off of her, hands on my shoulders, and looks me in the eyes. She's concerned. There's been a lot more concern lately. More than before. Matty peeks out from under the bed. Mom catches sight of her.

"What's going on guys?"

Just as I'm about to explain what happened with Drunky McDrunk-Pants, I see him lumber behind Mom. He's in the living room, headed toward the kitchen. Going for another beer no doubt. His arms are swinging back and forth as he slowly walks, or tries to walk. The sight of it all reminds me of that picture of Big Foot that someone took. We all know the one, the blurry one. Some people say it isn't real, some say it is.

Well, I just saw Big Foot in my living room, so take that doubters! Everyone's invited! Come see the stinky Sasquatch live, drunk and in person! I can charge admission and have that Batmobile in no time!

Apparently, my eyes tell Mom everything she needs to know. She looks over her shoulder, he's gone. In the kitchen. She pushes me back into the bedroom and quietly asks, "Did something happen with Chris?"

I want to answer yes. I want to tell her that I've tried giving Chris "a chance", and I'm done giving him chances.

Why won't she stop giving him chances? I don't like living with a caveman!

I'm in my head too much, my silence is giving Mom an answer. Matty isn't speaking up, so Mom is beginning to fear the worst.

"Guys. You have to talk to me," the worry in Mom's voice is heartbreaking.

Stupid Chris is literally ruining everything. Mom has never been this way. We've never been this way.

I finally find the courage, "Chris scares us."

A brief moment passes where I have no clue what Mom is thinking, and for once, I'm not thinking. Weird. That doesn't happen often.

"Okay. Okay, babies. Mamma's gonna fix this okay?"

Matty is quick to respond now, "Okay Mommy."

Me, I'm not so quick. Normally I would say, "Okay," and that would be that. But something… something is different with Chris.

Chris has some kind of power over Mom. Some kind of spell. What is it? I honestly can't see what it is. Why is he so special? Is this love? If this is love, I hate love. Love is worthless. Love is a blurry picture of Sasquatch. Some people swear by it and some people swear against it. Adult life is stupid. Why do they want us kids to grow up? The world makes so much more sense to me right here and now. The things they do is what don't make sense. "GROW UP!" they say. Well, I say, "YOU GROWN DOWN!"

My silence gets to Mom.

"Honey. I promise. Okay?"

"Okay," I respond reluctantly. It's not okay. I don't know how she's gonna "fix this."

This is Chris. Can she fix Chris? Just get rid of him!

Mom hugs us both and heads for the door. She looks back at us with a hopeful grin and then closes the door behind her as she leaves. Matty and I stay silent, listening.

Is she going to "fix it" now? I don't want to be out there if not. Honestly, I don't want to be out there if Chris is out there. See what he's done? He's made our house a place we don't want to be in. Geez.

Honestly, Chris wasn't bad at first. Yeah, I didn't want him around at the beginning, but that was because I felt like he was taking Mom from us. I felt like it was closing the door on Dad for forever. Matty and I started getting used to him though. We had fun from time to time, but things slowly got worse. I don't think we realized it was happening. I mean, it wasn't like there was a moment when things took a sudden turn. He just started drinking more and more… and more.

I remember the first time I saw him drink a beer was at dinner one night. He and Mom explained that it's okay to "have a cold one" with a meal when you're "grown". Mom never needed "a cold one" before. Was she not "grown" before Chris? Then one cold one turned to two or three, and not just at dinner. Jump to today where he plowed through God knows how many. Seems like he always has a beer in his hand. He must be really "grown" now. I mean he must be as grown as you can possibly get! He must be the grown-est.

We can hear Mom's muffled voice in the other room. It's hard to tell if she's in the living room or the kitchen. I can't understand what's being said, but Chris mumbles something. Silence. Chris mumbles something else. Silence. Both start mumbling together, louder. I could probably make out what's being said if they weren't mumbling over the top of each other.

Matty looks at me, "Can we go back to the Fortress of Solitude?"
"Yeah, let's go," I reply.

I may not be much help to Mom. She seems to have made her own decision with Chris, but I can at least be here for my sister. I can make sure she feels safe. We crawl back under my bed.   The mumbles are getting louder. I can make out words now. Some of them are "adult" words.

Chris. Boy, he's a gem, isn't he?

I pick up where I left off in the comic I was reading to Matty.   I don't want her to hear what's happening. To be honest, I don't really want to hear Chris' voice. It's kind of a win-win, reading the comic aloud.

A loud noise interrupts my reading. Something glass breaks. A kitchen drawer opens and slams closed. That's an unmistakable noise. Keys jingle as stomping footsteps walk the length of the house. The front door opens and slams closed, which rattles the walls. I stop reading. Silence. A moment passes, a long moment. Matty and I remain quiet. A soft tap on our door breaks the silence. It's Mom.

We crawl out from under the Fortress and I open the door. Mom must've locked it on her way out like I did. For protection. What was she expecting to happen? I open the door and Mom's there. She's been crying. I can tell. She's making herself stand brave, and honestly, I appreciate the effort because I'm dang near all out of brave. I've been using up all mine for both Matty and myself.

"You guys want pizza for dinner?" She asks.

Of course we do! What kind of question is that?!

I smile at her, she smiles at us. The air seems breathable again. The beer fog left when Chris did. We step out into the living room and Mom grabs the phone. She knows the number to Pizza Hut by heart.

I grab a trash bag from the kitchen and start picking up Chris' mess. Matty joins me.

There has to be like, twenty empty cans lying on or around the couch. Geez, they stink. How could anyone want to drink something that smells so horrible? I don't get it.

I hear Mom order two large pepperoni pizzas. Oh, man. I'm ready for that cheesy, saucy, pepperoni-y goodness! I didn't realize it was this late. We didn't get our after-school snack, and I'm pretty confident we've gone past the normal dinner time. My stomach is now threatening me. Matty is singing to herself as she twirls around the living room. I tie a knot in the trash bag filled with cans and let it drop next to the couch. Mom emerges from the kitchen. One of her eyes is really red. Earlier I thought it was because she was crying. I don't think that now.

"You okay Mom?" I ask.

"I'm fine," she assures, "Just bumped my eye. I'll be okay."

Nope. I don't buy it. I've been hit in the eye with a baseball before and that looks very close to what happened to me. Mom assures me, several times over, that she's fine, it was an accident. She tells me not to worry. She also informs Matty and me that Chris will be staying at his mom's house for a little while. The pizza comes and we eat all of it. Two large pepperoni pizzas – gone! We watch TV together and play a board game called Operation. And now it's bedtime. I can't sleep. I keep thinking about Mom's eye. I remember a few weeks back she wore sunglasses for a few days. Anytime I asked about it she'd just sing the song, "I wear my sunglasses at night, so I can, so I can see..." It was irritating and funny at the same time. I eventually dropped it.

The dots are connecting now. Ben didn't start that fight on Matty's birthday. It was Chris. Chris hit Ben. Chris hit Mom.

A wave of anger flushes over me. I don't know what to do with it. I'm restless and Matty must sense it because she starts singing to me. It's the song she made up. Her sweet voice soothes me, calms me. My eyes are getting heavy. I guess I am pretty tired.

EIGHT

The next morning we're awakened by Mom telling us to get up and get ready for school. Man, does my bed feel like the most comfortable thing in the world. I don't want to move, but I do. Reluctantly, I stumble out of bed and to the bathroom. I didn't shower last night, so I better hop in this morning.

The warm water is nice. I imagine I'm in the tank Wolverine was in when he was in the Weapon X facility. A bang on the door startles me.

"HURRY UP! I GOTTA PEE!" Matty screams.

I don't respond right away as I start my hustle to "rinse, lather repeat". My lack of response is Matty's cue to yell again. At least that's what she sees it as.

"DID YOU HEAR ME?!" BANG! BANG! BANG!

"YES!" I yell back, "GIVE ME A SECOND! I'M GOING AS FAST AS I CAN!"

I quickly rinse myself off, shut off the water and toss a towel around me. I open the door and my sister busts in, nearly knocking me over. I barely close the door before she's pants'd herself and is assuming the position.

"Geez! Let me close the door first!"

Her only response, "You've made it all steamy in here! It's too hot!"

I smile at her misery and close the door to let her sit in the heat. I make my way to my bedroom and throw on some clothes. I head to the kitchen.

Foooood. Mom's getting ready for the day herself, so I'll just grab some cereal, or better yet, waffles!

I throw some in the toaster and wait. When you're waiting on something, watching the timer, it takes forever. I feel like I could have toasted some waffles, thrown syrup on them and have eaten them by the time these suckers are done.

Is something wrong with this toaster?

Matty strolls into the kitchen, "Whatcha eatin'?"
"Waffles." My gaze is ever steady on the toaster.
"There any Pop-Tarts?" She asks.
"No. Remember yesterday?"

*I shouldn't have said that. I
don't want to remember yesterday. I
don't want her to remember yesterday
either.*

"Cocoa Puffs?" She seems unaffected. Good.
"I don't know," I respond, "Look."

She doesn't look. She just keeps asking me like I'm the keeper of all breakfast foods!

"How about Frosted Flakes?"

***GOOD   GRIEF!   THIS
TOASTER! THESE QUESTIONS!***

MY PATIENCE!

I turn to Matty and point at the cupboard we keep the cereal in, "Would you just look for yourself?!" She shrugs and climbs the countertop.

CLICK-CLICK!

FINALLY!

I grab the flaming hot waffles from the toaster and plop them on a plate waiting nearby. Matty has found a satisfactory cereal selection and is climbing down from the counter.

"Can you grab me the syrup?" I ask.

She hops down, "*Sorry*. I was already on my way down." She can be so sarcastic sometimes.

"Already on your way? I asked before you jumped!"

She smiles her ornery smile. I shake my head and grab the syrup for myself. I proceed to drown my waffles in the maple-y goodness. As we eat, Matty hums and kicks her legs under the table. Mom pops in after a couple of minutes. Putting earrings in she says, "Okay guys! Finish up and brush those teeth of yours. We're outta here in 5!"

She's managed to do a pretty good job of concealing the now black eye. She shoots me a smile as I'm staring at her. I can't help but smile back. She's pretty and she's my Mom. She sure is strong.

Mom drops us off at school, and school is… school. Nothing particularly eventful happens. We ride the bus home. The entire ride I'm quiet. Charles and Matty are yammering on about something. I pop in from time to time to contribute to the conversation, but I'm not in it. I keep thinking about what will happen if Chris is there when we get home. I know Mom said that he won't be around for a couple of days, but I just have this feeling. My stomach is sick. It's like when you drink milk and then go play outside in the summer heat. Nauseated.

The bus stops at our house. No El Camino. A wave of relief hits me. Good. I don't know how to deal with someone like Chris, to be honest, and I don't know what I'll do the next time I see him.

> *I hope I never see him again. He doesn't deserve my Mom. I hope my Mom knows that. Stupid Chris. I knew all along. Stupid Chris. I wish I wasn't just a kid. I'd show him. I'd make him wear sunglasses at night. Stupid Chris.*

I unlock the door and we walk into the house.

"Home alone!" Matty calls. "Let's jam some music!"

"I don't know," I reply. "We should just do our homework and wait for Mom. We can jam when she gets home."

She pays zero attention to my concern. She's over by the stereo picking out her "jams". That uneasy feeling in my stomach is back. All the stereo equipment is Chris'. It's expensive. He's never been one to share either.

"I really don't think we should be messing with all that," I warn.

Matty comes back, "It's fine! Mom said Chris is away."

"At least be careful," I reply.

I can't get over this feeling. I could blow chunks right here, right now, all over the carpet. I just need to calm down. It's fine. I'll just go splash some cold water on my face.

I make my way to the bathroom and turn the faucet on. I cup my hands together and let the water run into them and fill up my palms. I lift my hands and bury my face in the water. I dry myself with the hand towel nearby, and I breathe. Deep breaths. I hate throwing up. I hate throwing up more than I hate Stupid Dog, more than I hate missing my 'toons. It's the worst.

Wait... where's the music?

I open the door and Matty is standing there, wide-eyed, in shock, holding a broken tape case.

"I set the case on the floor and put the tape in," she starts, "but then I stepped back and…"

She doesn't finish. She doesn't have to. It's obvious that she stepped on the case. There's absolutely no fixing it. I take what's left of it from her hands and walk it over to the stereo. I place the remains on top.

"We'll tell Mom when she gets home. Let's go to our room and do our homework," I say with finality. Matty concedes.

We're in the zone. Homework is getting done. There are a few questions that each of us leave blank as we'll have to get Mom to help us when she gets home. Mom usually isn't long. We get home about 3:30 and she's usually home by 4:30. So, no big deal.

The front door opens and closes. Matty pops up, eager to greet Mom. She races into the front room.

"Mommy…"

Her voice trails off. I get up from the ground where I was finishing up my reading assignment for the evening and make my way to the door. Matty is just standing there. I step up behind her to see what's got her so silent.

Chris.

His unmistakable broad back is to us. He's examining the lifeless body of his cassette tape case. Even though we didn't make a noise, he spins around as if he heard us, or maybe he caught wind of us? His jaw is locked and it sounds like he's growling. His shoulders are moving up and down with his heavy breathing. He's finally made the transformation into what he's really been all along. He still looks like a man, but I know what he really is inside. Not like the kind you see in movies. Worse. A Monster.

The Monster takes a step forward and I step in front of Matty. I may only be half his size, but he's going to have to go through me first, the Champion of Cry Baby Road. He takes another step, panting. I almost expect him to start drooling any second now. Nearly every monster in every movie drools at some point. It's got to be coming. He takes another step. With it he breathes, "Who-," another step, "Broke-," another step, "My-", another step, "Case?"

There are no more steps left. He's now towering over my sister and me. I'm paralyzed, gripped with fear. I can feel Matty's trembling body tucking into my back. I have to push back a little as she's edging me closer to The Monster.

"I SAID WHO BROKE MY-"

"I did," I interrupt. I don't want to, but this poor excuse for a man likes to hit women. If he would hit my Mom, the sweetest woman on Earth, what would he do to my sister? No. Not today Monster. The words taste like vomit when they leave my mouth. Half of me regrets saying it. Half of me stands taller because of it.

My eyes are set on his. There's so much hatred in his eyes. How can someone become this? How does someone allow themselves to become the villain? His eyes, if they could glow red I bet they would. He's trying to kill me with his vision, I just know it.

The Monster lets loose and kicks me right between the legs. He kicks so hard that it lifts me off the ground. The blow knocks Matty back a couple of steps. Pain surges through my body. As the pain rushes in, all the breath I have in me escapes. I can't breathe. I hit the ground. I can't move. I can't breathe. I lay there feeling like I'm going to die. Am I?

"NEVER TOUCH MY STUFF AGAIN!" The Monster lingers, hovering. I blackout.

I wake to my Mom. She's frantic, "Baby! Baby! Are you okay?!"

Matty is crying. I'm having a hard time keeping my eyes open.

"Sweetie, I need you to say something!" Mom cries with her panic-stricken voice.

My eyes open and I see Mom. Just her being here makes me feel a little better. I think I can muster up some strength.

"I uh-"
"Baby, I need you to tell me what happened," She pleads.

I take in my surroundings a second. My mind is still swimming. I'm honestly not too sure what happened. Matty is still crying, but she looks unharmed. Good.

All I can get out is, "Chris."

"Chris did this to you?"

Mom straightens up. She looks at Matty. "Chris did this?"

She must be in shock because she's not saying much of anything. I'm not any help because I currently don't even know how to say much of anything other than The Monster's name. Stupid Chris. Stupid Monster. Mom grabs my sister and pulls her in close to me. She hugs us both, "I am so sorry."

She cries. Matty cries. I cry. She pulls back and looks me over, "I need to get you to the hospital." And as movie timing would have it, The Monster walks right through the front door at that very moment.

Mom immediately looks at us, fear in her eyes, "You two get in your room and lock the door now."

Oddly enough, I'm strengthened. Strength hits my legs and before I can even think to stand up, I'm standing. I'm completely aware. I don't understand and there is no possible way I can explain it, but I go with it. I motion for Matty to get in the room. I close the door just as Mom commanded. I lock the door as quick as I can and turn to Matty,

"Into the Fortress. NOW." I say, a little more sternly than intended.

We waste no time. We're both under the bed in record time. I pull blankets and pillows close and tight to my side. No flashlight and comics this time. Now, being completely conscious and aware, everything is catching up to me. The Monster obviously left. He wasn't here when Mom got here.

Poor Matty, all alone.

I turn to her, "Did he hurt you?"
She shakes her head, "He left after he kicked you."

Oh yeah. He kicked the crap out of me.

Suddenly I'm aware of how sore I am. A loud crash from the front room pulls my attention away. The Monster is roaring, and by the sound of it, completely trashing the house. Every once in a while Mom whimpers something. I want to go defend my Mom, but I remember how defending my sister ended. Matty pulls in close to me. With every yell, scream, thud, bang or crash she pulls in tighter. Her body is shaking. She's terrified.

I'm absolutely scared out of my mind, but that same strength that stood me to my feet is now making me brave. My mind is clear. It's the strangest thing and there is absolutely no way I can explain it.

The Monster and Mom are yelling at each other through crashes and sounds of destruction. I'm fighting off tears because I know my Mom is getting beat up. I don't know what to do. My throat burns and it feels like there is a basketball in there. The volume on the brawl drops drastically, but not completely. The Monster is choking my Mom.

He's gonna kill her.

My heart is pounding in my eyes now and I feel like I can't breathe. All of a sudden, I hear someone call my name. I've never heard this voice before in my life, but it also sounded very familiar. The Voice is peaceful and oddly calms me. I know it wasn't Matty, but I can't help myself. I have to ask.

I nudge her, "Did you say my name?"

She looks at me, wide-eyed and shakes her head. It wasn't her. It wasn't Mom or The Monster, they're fighting it out in the other room. It was literally in my ear. And just like that, I hear the Voice say my name again. It's the loudest, and yet somehow, most quiet voice I've ever heard.

I got kicked too hard. That's what it is. Something's damaged. Something's off. I'll go to the doc and they'll say, "You see, getting kicked too hard in the crotch, well that'll make you hear voices. Take two of these pills every day for the rest of your life and you'll be fine!"

The Voice interrupts my rabbit trail thought process. Maybe my hearing is off? Maybe I hit my head earlier?

I nudge my sister again, "You say my name?"
"No!" she whispers loudly.

She's probably thinking, there's a Monster in the next room and now my brother is hearing voices! Great!

The Voice speaks again.   This time with instructions.   This is the strangest thing that's ever happened to me, but it's completely undeniable.

"Go to the neighbor's house. The way is open."

I'm completely propelled to spring into action and do just as the Voice is instructing.   Oddly, as the Voice speaks I hear it, but see what it's saying at the same exact time.   I can't explain it and I know I sound completely wacko trying to.   I decide to just run with it.   I know exactly who "the neighbors" are.   When the Voice said "neighbor's house" I saw Bill and Felicia.   I saw their faces. I saw their house. That same strength from earlier is the same strength propelling me from under my bed. I grab Matty's hand and begin to army crawl.

"What are we doing?!" She demands, terrified.

"We're going to Bill and Felicia's house," I reply with confidence.

Maybe my confidence is enough to convince her. Maybe she heard the Voice too. Either way, she nods her head and I turn to the bedroom door. It's open. It's wide open. It wasn't before. I know, because I closed the door and locked it before we crawled into the Fortress of Solitude. I know I locked it. I remember the words the Voice spoke earlier, "The way is open."

I grab Matty by the hand and we start running. We clear our room and sprint passed Mom's room. Her door is closed. She managed to wrangle The Monster into that room somehow. At this point, I don't even know if she's alive. The house is a wreck, but the front door is wide open, just like our bedroom door. "The way is open." The words run back across my mind.

We blast out into the night air.

How much time has passed?
Geez! What time is it?

I keep the pace. No time to stop for the bikes. Gotta keep running. Matty is right on my heels. I haven't let go of her hand. I won't. The air is crisp, kind of chilly. It's burning my lungs, but I'm not letting up. Not until we get to our neighbor's house.

We turn into their driveway at a full sprint and head straight for their door. My foot hits their doorstep and immediately Felicia opens the front door. It's like she was looking for us, waiting for us.

What the crap? How?

I don't say anything. I'm panting.

"Do you two need to stay the night?" she asks.

> *How? How does she know? Did Mom call her?   But how would Mom know what the Voice told me to do? Did the Voice talk to Felicia like it did me? Maybe it told her we were coming? I don't know.*

I don't care. We do need to stay the night. I nod my head, still trying to catch my breath. Felicia smiles and motions for us to enter, "I'll get you guys some blankets and pillows."

NINE

The sharp pains from last night's blow to the crotch made it difficult to sleep last night. Didn't keep me awake, just woke me every time I moved. Matty sang me to sleep. Her song has become extremely comforting to me for some reason. I wanted to tell her about the Voice. But I didn't. I don't know if I will. I don't want to talk about any other part of last night. I just want to forget about it and move on. She's still asleep. Seems like Bill and Felicia are too. I'll just lay here until someone else 'wakes me up'. I wonder if Mom made it out.

Maybe she's...

A soft knock at the door interrupts my thoughts. I turn to try and listen. Felicia says something. So I guess she's up. Maybe she just didn't want to wake us? That's nice of her. And just like that, all the pain in my body leaves. It's replaced with pure joy and relief as Mom pokes her head into the living room where we're laid out on the couches. I throw the blankets off and rocket to her open arms. I can't hold back the tears. I don't want to. Feels like all the fear and stress of last night and all the times before are leaving with them. Mom holds me tight and cries as well. We just hold each other and sob. Mom pulls back, wipes the tears from my face and then hers. She smiles her beautiful smile that's now a little bruised and busted.

Chris. I hate Chris. Forget Chris! Mom is here now!

"Let's wake Matty and go get some breakfast," she whispers.

I nod. Food of any kind sounds good. Mom wakes Matty by shaking her shoulder. As soon as she notices Mom's the one doing the waking she shoots off the couch just like I did. We all hold each other close and cry.

Man, I'm glad Mom's okay.

We load up in the car and pull out onto the road. Everyone is silent. We pass our house. I'm honestly a little surprised it's still standing, the way things seemed to carry on last night. The Monster's car is gone. That's not as comforting as I want it to be. It just means that he's lurking somewhere else. Hopefully in another town, or state, or country, or planet. Yeah. We'll go with planet. He's not human anyway.

"Mom, we're late." I point to the clock on the dash. It's 9:35 am!

"Yeah, well you guys are going to take a day off from school," she explains. Her eyes still on the road. Her voice is hushed. I realize she wasn't whispering earlier. Her voice is strained. Probably from when she was choked.

UGH!   I HATE THE MONSTER!

I need to calm down. Anger helps nothing.

Matty is elated to be missing school. She's bouncing around in the backseat, chipper. I, however, know something is up. We don't 'take a day off' in the middle of the week.

"Mom," I start.
"It's okay baby. I'll explain everything after we eat. Okay?"

I'm good with that for now. We pull into the diner, park and get out. I'm slow to move. This is a whole new level of sore. Even more so than the day after Seaver Park Hill. It feels worse than riding on a bike seat with no padding.

"Sweetie…"

"I'm fine Mom." I keep walking. I can't be any worse than her! And if she's going to keep walking then

I'm going to keep walking! She nods and then caresses the back of my head.

We sit at a booth and order all kinds of breakfast. We eat like it's Thanksgiving dinner: Breakfast Edition. Pancakes, bacon, eggs, sausage, toast, hash browns, orange juice. I could name the entire menu and it's sitting right in front of us on this very table. I bet the table is struggling to hold the weight of it all. Eating helps our mood. It usually does for me.

"We're going to go stay with Grandpa and Grandma for a while," Mom states without looking up from her coffee.

"Yay!" Matty barely manages to pelt out before cramming more food into her face.

I'm more skeptical. I know something is up. "For how long?"

"Oh, I don't know," Mom responds. " For a little while."

Hmmm, 'a little while.' "So we'll drive back and forth to school?"

This'll get her. She's serious about education. This'll get an answer out of her. I'm shocked we're missing a random day of school. There's no way we miss an entire week for no reason!

"No school this week. You'll make up the work."

I choke on some OJ. It nearly comes out my nose! "Mom. What the crap is going on?" It came out before it even cleared my mind. Mom doesn't like it when I say 'crap' at the table. Oops.

"Language young man."
"Sorry."
"Just finish your breakfast and I'll tell you everything on the way."

I don't respond. What am I supposed to say? She's made up her mind that she's not saying anything until after we eat. Patience isn't my strong suit. I want to plow through my food to speed up the process, but I know my shoveling won't speed up Matty, or Mom. And Mom seems to be taking her sweet time over there pushing her dang eggs around with a fork.

JUST EAT EM!
EAT SO WE CAN KNOW WHAT'S GOING ON!!!

Finally. In the car. On the road. Leaving town. I slowly turn to Mom. She knows what's coming. She shakes her head with a slight grin.

"You're so persistent."
"Yep. Now tell me."

Her eyebrows lift in a way that reminds me I forgot my manners.

"Please?"

Her eyebrows drop. Whew. Okay. We're good.

"Okay you two," she starts.   She adjusts the rearview mirror so she can see Matty in the back.   She continues, "I have a lot of your things packed in the trunk. I want to make sure you're as comfortable as possible at Grandpa and Grandma's house."

"What toys did you pack?" Matty asks.
"I grabbed what I could," Mom responds.
"My Power Rangers?"
"Yes, but I couldn't get your playset."
"It's the Command Center Mom. Why?" Matty asks, a little agitated.
"I didn't have time or enough room in the trunk."

Mom is growing tired of the back and forth with Matty concerning her toys. I can tell. Matty can't, or she doesn't care. I didn't want to ask her what she brought of mine. Actually, I did want to ask. I wanted to ask her everything, but I didn't want to cause any more of what Matty was stirring up.

Matty continues plowing, "What about my Catwoman, and my coloring books and crayons and my – "
"Honey, you'll just have to see it all when we get there okay?"

She looks at me. I look at her. "I got your GameBoy. I wasn't sure about everything you wanted, so I just grabbed a few things. I'm sorry." With that, she turns her attention back to the road. Her eyes beginning to well up.

What is she sorry about? Why did she 'grab what she could'? She 'didn't have enough time'? What is this? I don't even know what questions to ask. I thought she was going to explain? Something is up. Something is weird about all of this.

"We'll be back before Saturday right? We've got to be at Tommy's by 10 am at the latest," I inform.
"You may have to watch your cartoons at your Grandparents this weekend," she responds.
"What? Why? We're missing school and we're missing the guys? Why?"
"There's something I have to do, and it could take some time."
"What do you have to do Mommy?" asks Matty.
"We're close to Grandpa and Grandma's house. We'll talk there."

She keeps putting it off. Something's up and I don't like it! I stare at her and she pretends to not see it. She wipes a tear from her eye as it falls. She's fighting crying. My Mom is usually a pretty strong woman, so for her to cry just because we're visiting Grandpa and Grandma is weird.

We pull into my grandparents' driveway. As we pull in, both of them walk out onto the porch and down onto the sidewalk to greet us. We've barely parked before

Matty busts out the door and bounds over to them with open arms.   Man, I love my Grandparents.   They are literally the nicest and sweetest people on earth.   Grandpa can fix literally anything. Grandma can literally play the piano like a literal pro and literally cook even better! Literally.

I could easily weigh 1000 pounds by the end of the week!

I open my door and get out. Both are smiling at me which makes it impossible to not smile back. So I smile my big awkward smile and give them hugs.

Grandpa speaks up first, "Grab your stuff and take it to the guest room."

Mom pops the trunk. I step around and see three duffle bags and our pillows from our beds. I grab my pillow and two of the bags. Matty grabs her pillow and the remaining bag. Mom closes the trunk and we make our way past Grandma who pats us both on the head. She seems sad. Wonder why?

"You okay Grandma?" I ask.
"You bet. Take your stuff in," she responds with a soft smile.
As we enter the house, we're met by the smell of pumpkin bread. Matty and I look at each other with hungry smiles.

"Oh, man! Grandma's been baking!" I exclaim with too much enthusiasm.

We hurry to the guest room and drop our stuff on the guest bed. Matty unzips her bag, all clothes. I unzip my bag, clothes. I wouldn't unzip the other bag if I knew it was Mom's. Personal space and all, but I carried it in and I know it's not clothes. I unzip it and it's full of toys and my GameBoy. I look at Matty, who seems none-the-wiser. Where's Mom's stuff? These were the only bags. There were no others in the trunk or in the back seat. Just these three and our pillows. I quickly stand and make my way hurriedly back outside. Matty follows. She's picked up on my urgency.

"What's wrong?" she asks.
"I don't know." I have a feeling, but I don't know. Not for sure.

Mom's leaning up against the car. She's crying. Grandma is crying. Grandpa is usually a rock, but he's looking a lot like a soft rock at the moment. If there is such a thing? Clearly, we interrupted a conversation being had. I don't care. I want answers and there is no more friggin' places to drive to! She can't say, 'I'll explain when we get there', anymore! WE ARE THERE!

I look Mom straight in the eyes, "Where's your stuff?"

She swallows hard. Her lip quivers.

"What's happening? You said you would tell us," I demand. I purposefully left the manners off this time. I'm done with all that for the moment and I don't care if I get scolded for it.

Mom steps over to Matty and me and places a hand on each of our shoulders.

"I have to go for a while. You are going to be staying here with your Grandparents."
"How long?" I quickly demand.
"I'm not sure. You'll have to finish the school year here. I…"
"What?! Why?" I demand. I'm not letting her get away without explaining this time.

A new school?! What about Tommy and Jason and Charles?!

"I have to take care of some things and it will take some time."
"What things?!" My tone is rising and I'm fighting back tears.
"I can't say right now. It'll have to wait until you get older."

Older?!

Did my mom just forget everything? I feel like I'm 55 years old at this point. She can't explain until I'm OLDER? Everything that has happened in the last several weeks and she's leaving us? All that pain and fear and she's leaving us? And she won't even explain why? I'm furious.

"Fine." That's all I can say as a tear streaks down my cheek. I don't even know what else I could say. I don't have the energy to wrestle it out of her and the longer I stand here doing this, the more likely it is that I'll just start crying.

"Please don't be angry," Mom pleads.

"Why would I be angry?" I clearly am. You see, the words she just used, 'I have to go away for a while,' those are the same words my Dad said to me when he left. And then, just like that, it shoots out before I even think, "First Dad leaves and now you. Why would I be angry?"

My words, a dagger to my Mom's heart. She starts sobbing. I feel awful. I want to apologize, but before I can she bends down, hugs us both and turns to leave. Matty grabs ahold of Mom, sobbing. Both of them are sobbing. Grandpa has to pull Matty off of Mom. This moment is the worst. This is more awful than getting kicked by the Monster. My heart is broken for my Mother. My heart is broken by my Mother. My heart is broken for my sister. I feel betrayed and alone. I feel abandoned.

We watch as Mom drives away. Who knows if we'll ever see her again? I know she's going back to our house. The house she probably almost died in last night.

Our Grandparents hold us tight as we cry every
last tear we have in us, right there on their front sidewalk.

TEN

I pick up my pillow and out falls my Batman and Batmobile. Tears begin to well up, but I fight them back the best I can.

> *I wonder if I'll ever get to see Tommy again? Or if I'll see Jason or Charles? I don't want to start a new school. I don't want to make new friends. I have the best friends.*

Matty and I lay down in our new bed, in our new room that once was the guest bed in the guest room at Grandpa and Grandma's house. Our stomachs are full of pumpkin bread. Which I do have to admit, helps a lot. I wish I could apologize to Mom. I wish that what I said wasn't the last thing I'd said to her. I wish I said, "I love you" or "I understand." Even though I don't understand. I wish I hadn't compared her to Dad. She's never been anything like him. I hope she's okay.

Matty interrupts my self-inflicted mental beating, "Stop thinking so much."

"Sorry."

There's a long pause between us as we lie there in silence. I can tell Matty's thinking something. I also know that she wants me to talk to her about it since she interrupted my thoughts. She probably doesn't know how to put words to it. The last 24 hours have been the most difficult 24 hours of our entire lives.

"I'm sorry," she says, interrupting my thoughts yet again.
"For what?" I ask.
"All of this is my fault," she chokes out.

Matty's not one to cry without good reason, but when that reason is there she lets loose. Right now, all of this is as good a reason as any. Tears flow from her eyes, not the small little tears you can easily wipe away. These tears are like someone opened up some floodgates. I hug her tight and she cries into my shirt.

"None of this is your fault. Not one single bit."
"But... I..."   She tries to pull herself together. "But I broke the case!"

The sobbing kicks right back in. I didn't consider how much all of this was affecting her. I've been very much concerned with keeping her safe physically, but I didn't think about her emotions, her mind, her heart. I can't let her think that what happened to me, what happened to Mom, is her fault.

"All of this is that idiot's fault," I assure. I feel anger beginning to rise in me, so I need to try and check that if I'm going to continue. "Sure, you broke the case, but that was an accident. And, he deserves worse."

That's not helping.

"I mean, he's an adult and he makes his own choices. It's not our fault he's an idiot drunk!"

Matty hugs me tight and takes in a deep breath. It's choppy.   Crying hard makes breathing difficult sometimes. She wipes her face with her hands and then looks at me.

"You sure? He hurt you. He hurt Mom."
"I'm one hundred percent sure," I answer without hesitation.   "One hundred percent sure he's an idiot!"

Matty laughs and slaps me on the arm.

"Oh! Ouch!" I cry playfully.
"Shut up!" she answers.

We lay still as the quiet washes back over us. The air is a lot less heavy now. She's been holding that in. I hate that. She doesn't hold things in. I do, but I can. I guess. Well, come to think of it, I don't want to hold things in either.

Maybe I should open up too? Nah. Not now. I need to be the strong one right now.

"Want me to sing the song?"
"Yes."

Matty sings and I drift off.

Surprisingly, the next few weeks move pretty quickly. We enroll in our new school. Matty finds a friend almost immediately. Well, honestly, I'm not sure Matty had much say in the matter. Her friend Randy is about the loudest, most out-there girl (or person, for that matter) I've ever met. And that's saying a lot because Matty is my sister. When those two are together every eardrum in the room is begging for mercy.

Randy has extremely long, extremely straight brown hair. It's super shiny. It almost makes you want to touch it to see what it's made of. She goes into ninja chop mode any time anyone tries though. I've never tried because I value my life. Still wanna. Her eyes are blue and her smile is huge. It kind of reminds me of the Joker, but I would NEVER tell her that. I'm too afraid of what she and Matty would do in retaliation. She's cool though.

She and Matty became best friends immediately. I'm glad for them. Matty needs a best friend. I'm not fitting in as easily. The new school is bigger than our last school. It's hard to pick out who is who. The jocks are always easiest to spot, but where are my Ghostbusting, Power Ranger Morphin, Teenage Mutant Ninja, X-Men lovin', Batmobile driving nerds at? I miss Tommy and the gang. Matty doesn't know, but I bring my Batmobile with me to school every day. I keep it in my pocket. It's stupid, I know, and childish, but I need to feel close to something right now. I try calling the guys and I get them every once in a while, and it's great talking with them, but they are busy out doing what we all used to do together. It's hard knowing I'm not a part of that anymore.

I spend a lot of my time drawing and sketching. I'm honestly pretty proud of some of my work. I haven't shown anyone. Every once in a while I sketch something on the back of some of my school work and my teacher will write an encouraging note next to it. That's nice.

Mom's been calling. Man, has it been good to hear her voice. I apologized profusely for what I said and how I treated her. She acted as if nothing ever happened. She's sweet. It's been a while since we've seen her. She's supposed to be coming to see us in a couple of weeks. I don't know what that means. Maybe that's why I haven't tried to make friends? Maybe I'm hoping Mom just comes and gets us and we go back to life as usual. Without the Monster, of course.

"Hey man! You wanna play? We need one more to play 3 on 3." Bucky Johnson, a jock, one of THE Jocks, is asking me if I want to jump in with his other jock friends and play basketball. I do like basketball a lot, but I'm not their quality. I can promise that. But here I am. All lost in thought while Bucky and the other jocks stare at me.

"So you in?"
"Uh… yeah. I'll play."

What? Who said that? Who is talking out of my mouth right now? So I guess I'm playing.

"Cool. I'm Bucky. You're on my team with David there."

Bucky's a cool guy. He's unbelievably good at basketball, and I'm assuming all things sports. He seemingly has every pair of Michael Jordan signature basketball shoes that have ever been made. He's a tall and lanky African American kid. He's really fast and he can probably jump over the moon. Not literally, but maybe a cloud. This dude can jump! His "fro", as he calls it, always has a neon green pic in it. Always.

So we play, and it's fun. I'm surprisingly doing well! I've already made a couple of shots. Two for four, so I've got a 50% shooting average from the field. Not too shabby! Then the bell rings.

"Hey, good game man! Wanna play with us tomorrow?" Bucky chimes.
"Yeah," I respond.

"All right then! You be my Scotty Pippen! I'll be MJ of course!"

"Well, you've got the shoes!" I say, agreeing to the terms.

"All right, then Pip!" He says with a high five, then bolts off.

It's too bad we're not in the same class. I think we could be good friends. For the first time in forever, I can say I have a friend! I like that.

After school, Matty and I walk home. We live relatively close by, and though it's somewhat cold out, it's a nice day. Our options are to either walk now or wait an extra 40 minutes for Grandpa to come pick us up. So we walk!

"Randy said something funny today," starts Matty.

"Okay."

"You know Aaron Dinkle?"

Aaron Dinkle is in my grade, so he's above Matty and Randy, but EVERYONE knows who Aaron Dinkle is. He should probably be a couple of grades up, but I don't look down on that type of thing. Technically I should be in one grade higher myself. Aaron's a bully in a long line of bullies. I guess his brother is in High School and he's a bully there. And before that, his even older brother was a bully. The Dinkles. Hilarious name, terrible people.

"Yeah, I know Dinkle," I assure.

"Well, he was picking on one of our friends at recess, Gina."

"He was picking on a girl?" I shouldn't be shocked, but for some reason I am. Boys are not supposed to bully girls.

"Yeah. He made her cry. Then I told him to leave her alone, and I guess with me and Randy and Gina all there, he was scared of us or something, so he left."

"I'd be scared too," I say with a smile. "You and Randy are like Wonder Woman and Super Girl." Matty takes the compliment with a huge smile.

"So anyway! Randy tells us, after Aaron leaves, 'Well, I've gotta go take an Aaron and wipe my Dinkle!'"

We both lose it. I laugh so hard that we have to stop walking. I'm bent over holding my knees to keep myself up. That is literally one of the funniest things I've ever heard, and the fact that it was said about Aaron Dinkle just makes it so much funnier. That, plus butt and poop humor is my favorite. It's gross, I know, but it's hilarious.

Take an Aaron and wipe my Dinkle! Ha! So funny!

We arrive home in high spirits. Grandma is happy to see us, and surprise! Mom is on the phone for us! This day just keeps getting better and better! I let Matty talk first, but only because she managed to get to the phone before me. That's fine. I'll have a snack and wait. I have to stand close by so Matty doesn't lose herself in an eternal talkfest. If she starts revving up I can remind her that I need to talk to Mom too.

I down my snack and listen on as Matty rambles about events that have transpired since she last spoke with Mom. She tells mom about Randy and Aaron Dinkle, and we crack up laughing all over again.

> ***Take an Aaron and wipe my Dinkle! Hysterical!***

I can hear Mom's voice over the phone. I can't make out what she's saying, but I can hear her. It's a nice sound. I give Matty a few more minutes and then I wave to remind her of my existence. She gets the point and nods. She says her goodbyes and sends her love, then hands me the phone. Afterward, she grabs something from the fridge and then bounces off to our room.

"Hey, Mom!" I'm excited.
"Hey, kiddo! How are you?"
"I'm good. How are you?"
"Oh, just missing you. What's new?" she asks.
"I made a friend today!"
"Great news! And who is this friend?"
"Bucky! That's not his real name, but everyone calls him that. Even the teachers."
"Like how we call you Brother?"
"Yeah! We played basketball during recess. We're supposed to play again tomorrow."

"I'm happy for you!"

"You still coming this weekend?" I ask.

"Well honey, something's come up and I'm not going to be able to make it."

"Why? You said you were coming." I'm disappointed but trying hard not to let mom hear it.

"I know babe, and I'm very sorry. Next time I come I'll make it up to you. Promise."

"Why can't we just come home?"

"Honey…" Mom sighs. That's not a good sign.

"Why can't you tell me what's going on?"

"Chris has gone away honey and I've had to deal with all that. When you're older I can explain it better."

"Always when I'm older. You know I'm almost a teenager, right? You know I know things, right? I'm not a stupid little kid Mom."

"Oh honey, I know that and I'm not saying you are. These are all just very adult situations, and you are still a kid. Like it or not."

"Not."

"What?"

"You said, 'like it or not.' I said, 'not'."

Even though I'm dead serious, Mom begins to laugh. I guess that was funny to her. And now, because she's laughing, a smile starts to slowly creep onto my lips. I can't help it. But she won't stop! After a few seconds, I can't take it and I start laughing with her. It's not fair! I want to be mad!

"Okay… I promise I'll make it up to you, okay?"

"Okay mom," I agree reluctantly.

"You know, I can tell you've already grown up a lot in the last few weeks. I'm really sorry I'm missing it."

"You'll have to really make it up to me," I state through a grin. I know she can hear my grin because I can hear hers.

"Oh I will, will I?"

"Yeah, with pizza and movies and video games and – " Mom interrupts my list with more laughter. I really miss her.

ELEVEN

"Hey! Let's go fishing." Grandpa hands me a fishing pole.

"Do fish bite when it's cold outside?" I ask.

"Doesn't matter." Grandpa shoots me a smile and a wink.

So I guess this little trip isn't about the fishing then! Okay. I've been spending a lot of time with Grandpa; working on his truck, messing around in his garage, stuff that people call "manly". Everyone knows that that's not a point to be taken literally. There are lots of men in the world that don't do that sort of stuff and that doesn't make them any less of a man.

I guess today I'll be adding fishing-but-not-fishing to the list. For what it's worth, I really do like being with Grandpa and Grandma. Other than Mom and Matty, they are my favorite people in the world.

We load up in his truck that he's brought back to life more times than cats have lives, and pull out of the driveway. His truck smells like work. I can't explain what that smells like, maybe engine oil, sweat and black coffee? I don't know. But whenever I smell anything remotely close to that aroma I think of my Grandpa. He is always wearing pointy-toed cowboy boots. He has his work boots and then his dress boots. He's a work-hardened man. He's not hard, he just looks like he works hard. His blue eyes soften him up, though. He has Native American blood, so he stays tan year-round. He's not a very big guy, though he still has a commanding presence. His gray hair that's feathered back is often hidden by either a trucker cap or a cowboy hat.

"What's on your mind kid?" His eyes steady on the gravel road we've turned onto.

"I dunno. Mom, I guess."

"Yeah. You still playin' ball with your friends at school?"

"Yeah. Every day at recess we play. Bucky wants me to try out for the team next year."

"That's a great idea!"

"If I'm still here." My gaze is out my window, but I can feel Grandpa looking at me. He's silent.

"So the trick to catching a fish in early spring," Grandpa starts, interrupting the awkward silence, "is you've gotta use smaller bait. You can't use the lures you'd use in the summertime."

I appreciate him not pushing the conversation. I love my Grandpa. I know he knows that. We've had too many conversations in the last couple of months for him to not understand where I'm coming from. He's been there for me and Matty and I'm so thankful for that. He and Grandma have been great. They were there for us when we had problems sleeping at night and when we've needed help with homework. Even when Mom didn't come to

Christmas. She sent money. That made me so angry. I didn't care about getting crap! I wanted to see my Mom! It's been a ridiculously hard couple of months and they've been there every painful step of the way.

"So when you feel a nibble," Grandpa continues as we drive. I probably should have been listening.
"Don't jerk the line right away. Wait until the hook is set. Give it a couple of seconds and then pull up directly. Reel it in until you feel the fight back. When it starts fighting you keep that line tight and wait for it to tire. Once it does, you reel that puppy in!"

"I didn't know we were catching puppies!"

Grandpa turns to me, confused. I'm all smiles. Dumb joke I know, but it got him. He chuckles and then rubs the hair on top of my head.

We pull off the dirt road. "This is 'ole Marty Baker's land," he informs. As if I know who the crap Marty Baker is. I don't. Grandpa knows everyone, and everyone knows him. He's super popular. Grandma hates going to the grocery store with him. She claims that it takes three times the amount it should because he has to stop and talk to everyone. I don't think it's much of an exaggeration. I think it's fun to watch. Grandma's patience being tested is a funny sight to see. She's a very kind, loving woman, but it's hilarious when she's hit the, "Okay, I'm done", mark.

We pull up to a pond, get out and grab our fishing gear from the bed of the truck. We make our way to the edge of the shore.

Anyway, we walk up to the edge of the sh-river bank of the pond.

"I already set you up with a lure. Cast in and don't reel too fast. They won't chase it."

Grandpa casts in. I watch him for a moment. Wonder if the truck ride conversation was the real reason we came out. Sometimes I think Grandpa just needs an excuse to get away from everyone. Local Celebrity Grandpa. LCG.

"You gonna cast in?"

"Yep!" I exclaim louder than I should. He snapped me out of my inner thoughts and I just kind of blurted it out. It didn't shock him. He just put his finger up to his mouth, "Fish'll scare easy."

I cast out and begin to reel in.

"So," starts Grandpa.   Here we go.   Here's the reason. "The Voice been speakin' to you lately?"

I told Grandpa about The Voice a while back. I had to tell someone. The best part is he didn't think I was crazy. Grandpa thinks The Voice, get this, is God! I don't know why God would want to talk to me, but Grandpa said, "If God is talkin' to you that's b'tween you 'n Him. Don't no one else need to butt in."

"Not really."

The Voice, God, hasn't said anything since that night. But, the feeling I got when I heard The Voice say my name, I've felt that several times since. The best way to describe the feeling is a feeling of peace and rest and hope, all combined. It feels good. It feels a lot like love. I remember feeling it on the nights that were the hardest. I remember feeling it on Christmas when I hid in the closet and cried because Mom didn't come. I remember feeling it when I told Grandpa about The Voice for the first time. Maybe I'm crazy, but I don't care. I think Grandpa's right. This is between me and The Voice. If no one else in the world hears The Voice it doesn't discredit that I did. That I do.

Grandpa cuts in, "Well I'm sure if He has somethin' to say, He'll say it." I reel in and cast out again. Grandpa is about to say something else. I can tell.

"You ever talk to Him? He finally asks.
"Who?" I ask, "The Voice?"
"Yeah."

He's sold that The Voice is God. I think maybe I am too. Who else would be talking to me? The devil? The devil is the opposite of God in all the stories, right? If they even are stories. Over the last few months, all that stuff started to feel more and more real. Why would the devil save me? He's evil. Evil doesn't save. Evil is the Monster. I'm all too familiar with what evil can do. The Voice isn't that.

"Not really," I answer. "What would I say?"

"I dunno. Just talk. I guess." He reels in and casts out again

"Do you?" I ask.

"Do I what?"

"Do you talk to or hear from The Voice?" It just dawned on me that I've never asked my Grandpa if he ever has.

"Not a day goes by that I don't."

I stop reeling. I'm relieved and blown away at the same time. At least I'm not crazy! Unless, of course, it runs in the family or something. But my Grandpa, the wisest man I've ever known communicates with The Voice that saved my life. This is amazing! I'm not quite as alone as I thought I was after all!

Grandpa reels in and turns to me, "I think we've caught all we're going to today. What you think?"

I think we've casted out 3 times each total and there's no possible way we've been here long enough to say that. But again, I knew we were coming out here for something other than fish.

"I think so," I respond. I understand. At least I think I do. Grandpa hears from God out here, when he's working on his truck, when he gets alone.

We drive home. I can't help but feel that feeling, that presence of peace and hope as we drive home.

"Thank you for saving me," I whisper as I stare out the window.
"What's that?" Grandpa asks.
"I uh, I was just…"

Grandpa nods. He understands. I understand. We understand.

I look to Grandpa, "I think I'm going to try out for the basketball team next year."

A huge smile grows across Grandpa's sun-kissed face, "Is that so?" He rubs my hair as he did before. As he has a million times before.

> *If I ever start styling my hair, he's gonna have to stop that!*

We pull into the driveway and get out. As we walk into the house the smell of chocolate chip cookies greets us.

"Grandma taught me how to make her cookies! It's a secret though, and I'm not allowed to tell you how." Matty is beaming.

"Well, it's a good thing that I don't care how they're made, only that they are in my stomach!" I call as I push past her eagerly.

"Wash your hands!" Grandma calls as I rush to the cookies.

Twelve

"You should do one of me and Matty next!" insists Randy.

Matty and Randy have been watching me with many of my art endeavors lately. Grandma found out about my "gift" (as she calls it) by seeing my sketches and drawings on my school work. I wasn't expecting it at all when she woke me up one Saturday with an easel, canvas, paint, sketchbooks, all kinds of art supplies. She even made Grandpa clear out half the garage to give me a place to "use my gift". He parks his truck in his workshop now, but he doesn't seem to mind.

At first, I didn't want anyone watching me draw or paint or sketch, but I do have to say that I'm getting pretty good. So I don't mind as much now. I spend a lot of time in this garage. I kind of lose myself here.

"And you should make us warrior princesses!" Matty adds.

"Oh!   He should make us Mega Rock Star Goddesses!" Randy corrects.

"You guys think very highly of yourselves huh?" I toss over my shoulder as I continue. Neither of them pay much mind to my comment.

Grandma has been teaching Matty piano, so naturally, this means she will be the next BIG THING in music, according to her and Randy. I don't doubt that Matty can conquer the world, I do however doubt that she'll be doing it only knowing how to play "Mary had a Little Lamb" and basic chords. She'll get there, eventually.

"You know," starts Randy, "we're going to need someone to do all of our album artwork…"

I can feel Randy staring at the back of my head. That's a regular occurrence, so I'm used to it.

"You guys focus on the music and when you need me, I'll be here."

Randy squeals like I just agreed to take her to the ball. I know she has a crush on me. It's only a little bit obvious. She takes every opportunity to oh-so-lightly- drop clues and hints. I try to ignore it for the most part. She's Matty's best friend first of all. Second, she's younger than I am and lastly… I'm a little scared of her if I'm completely honest. I just enjoy having her and Matty around. They're "on my team" if that makes any sense.

Other than art, which does take up a ton of my free time, I've been playing ball with Bucky and David on the regular. They want me to join the track team to prep for next season, but I hate running. I don't mind it on the court because I'm focused on playing.

School is school. I'm glad it is. Things are feeling normal. I do still miss Tommy, Charles and Jason, but everything here has been good. It takes the sting out of it.

A knock on the garage door pulls me from my canvas. The garage door is usually half-open when we're in, so anyone that comes up usually just sticks their head under.

"Hey Pip! You in there?" calls Bucky as his head pokes under the door.

"Hey Bucky!" I answer.

"Ladies," Bucky nods at Matty and Randy as he limbos his way into the garage.

"Your Grandma said you were in here. You wanna go shoot some hoops? Bunch of us gettin' together down at the park."

"Right now?"
"Right now."
"I'll go ask."
"You painted that?" Bucky asks.

He's shocked. I forgot I don't share my art much. I guess I never told Bucky and the guys that I'm into art and not just ball.

"Yeah. I like to draw and paint and stuff," I admit nervously. Hope he doesn't think I'm a dork. I mean, I am one, but I hope he doesn't think I am.

"Dude, that's so cool, man!" We share grins and I run off to ask Grandma if I can go to the park. I find her in the kitchen, as per usual. Grandma loves to bake and cook and all things food. I tell her all the time that she should open a restaurant, but she always comes back with something about that taking the fun out of it for her. I think the kitchen is for Grandma what outdoors is for Grandpa. It's her zone, her space, her quiet place.

"Hey Grandma, you mind if I go to the park with the guys?" I hardly get the words out without drooling over the apple pies that she's preparing.   She's barely even started making them, but man I know the outcome. Matty and I with stomach aches because we've eaten too much.

"I don't mind, but you know Matty and Randy will want to go with you. You good with that?"
"That's fine," I answer. It is fine. I don't mind at all. The guys never seem to mind either. We're usually too focused on playing ball.

"Be back before dinner so you can wash up."
"Yes ma'am!"
"Love you, kid!"
"Love you too Grandma!" I call as I'm out the door to the garage.   That's where Mom gets it.   The overflowing love.   No complaints here!   I love hearing them say that they love me.

"Dang Pip! I still can't believe you painted this man!" Bucky is studying the canvas like he's an appraiser. "How long this take?" he asks.

"Oh, I'm not done yet," I inform. The landscape I'm working on isn't anything all that special. I saw Bob Ross do one.   The way he paints both inspires me and makes me want to quit painting all at the same time. Bucky seems legitimately impressed though, which is nice.

"You ready to rock?" I interrupt.

"Yeah, man! Let's do this! Great job on the painting man! You do anything else?" We take the conversation on the go.

"Yeah. I draw and paint and do all sorts of stuff all the time."

"You do any MJ?" he grunts as we scamper under the garage door. He means Michael Jordan, not Michael Jackson. I've done both though, so I could say, "yes", regardless.

"I have," I inform with a grin. I know what's coming.

"Dude! You gotta show me!"

I'm not too proud of my MJ, Michael Jordan. Though my MJ, Michael Jackson, turned out nice. I'll have to create some sort of excuse that'll delay Bucky long enough for me to try again.

"Okay," I answer.

WHAT? OKAY? Why didn't I just listen to myself? Geez! Maybe he'll forget. Maybe he'll forget long enough for me to take another whack at it. It'll probably take me a few hours. I might be able to have something for him to look at tomorrow, or if he can wait for school in a couple of days that would definitely give me the time I need. Let's shoot for Monday. Hopefully.

"Cool," Bucky replies. "I'll swing by in the morning to take a look!"

Crap.

"So we've got quite a few guys that are supposed to be at the park. Hopefully, we can do 5 on 5 and run full court!" Bucky says excitedly.

Bucky's dribbling a basketball between his legs with each step. He does it with ease, which is a tad irritating. I look like a moose trying to walk on ice when I try. Oh better yet! I look the way a baby deer looks when it's trying to take its first steps. I can dribble just fine, just not between my legs. That's cool though because I'm not really a ball handler. I usually play power forward - down low. Bucky calls it a "big man position". I call it a mercy position. I'm still not the caliber ballplayer he and the others are, so I'm down there to do my best to grab a rebound and maybe score from the block. Bucky's taller than I am anyway, so if anyone should be playing the big man position (according to size) it should be him.

The park is only a few blocks from my Grandparent's house. Not a long walk at all, and it's

143

relatively nice out. Spring is seemingly a little early this year; light jacket weather at worst. Matty and Randy are a few steps behind Bucky and me. Probably talking about boys, or their breakout album or something.

"So I think I'm gonna try out for the team next year," I inform Bucky.
"Dude! You should! We can play all summer long and get you ready! Run drills and all that stuff!"
"Drills?"
"Yeah, so you know how to play your position."

"Oh yeah. That's probably a good idea!" I honestly have no clue if this is a good idea or not. Drills. It's a plural word. That means there are more than just one or two of them. Probably should have had this information before stating I was going to try out. The park is loaded. There are two basketball courts, right beside a tennis court. All of them are completely full, packed. And wouldn't you know it, riding their bikes through one of the courts, messing up the game in session, are two of the three Dinkles.

Well great. I gotta run drills and deal with the Dinkles. I'm a universe away from strapping on a proton pack and going to buy comics and candy.

We join a group of guys on the court that's not being terrorized by the not-so-Dynamic Duo.

> *I shouldn't have even used that team's name in association with the*
>
> *Dinkles. I'm sorry Batman and Robin.*

"Hey Pip!" calls David.

The nickname that Bucky gave me stuck. So now I have two recurring nicknames in the same school; Pip, or Pippen, and Brother. I'm good with it. Though deep down inside I was kind of hoping, somehow, that I'd get the nickname, Cap.

You see in Marvel Comics, Bucky Barnes is Captain America's best friend. Since Bucky and I are becoming closer friends… forget it. I forget that I am a long way from Kansas, Toto. Or at least a long way from my Nerdy little universe I used to belong to. This one is filled with basketball, art and working on crap with Grandpa. I guess this is growing up?

"Hey Dave!" I respond. I almost forgot to. Lost in thought again.
"We've got next," he informs Bucky as we look on to the game in progress.
"We play winner or loser?" Bucky asks.
"Winner," confirms David.

The team in the lead is good. I sure hope I don't let the guys down. I scan the park for Matty and Randy.

With the Dinkles around I've got to make sure we're staying in the clear. Good. They've taken seats on the bleachers just off the courtside. There are a couple of other girls there from school that I'm sure they'll strike up conversations with. Now, where are the Dinkles?

I scan the other court where they had previously been. Not there. I quickly turn my attention to Matty and Randy, they're clear. I look to the tennis court, not there. Maybe they got tired of being themselves and they left to reflect on their poor choices and lifestyles?

Bucky taps me on the shoulder, "We're up Pip!"

We take the court and the best shooter on each team shoots for first possession. Bucky is the one shooting on our team. He shoots and he scores! Okay! The ball is ours to start. The court is packed, so we're only playing half-court instead of full like Bucky had hoped for. And instead of 5 on 5, we're playing 4 on 4. After a few baskets back and forth, I hear a noise that always throws me into action.

Matty is screaming. It's not the kind of screaming that sounds like laughter or fun, not surprise or startle, but one that I immediately recognize as something being vitally wrong. I spin from the game, my attention locked on the bleachers. Aaron Dinkle has Matty pinned to one of the seats. I spring into action without thought. There is literally nothing on my mind and I don't know if it's adrenaline, or maybe I've developed superhuman abilities as of late, but I've never run faster. I'm at the bleachers before I can even think about it. I hurdle the first two levels of bleachers and smash right into Aaron Dinkle, throwing him off my sister and up an entire level. I quickly scramble to my feet. Still no thoughts. My chest is broad and my arms are out, I'm in serious defense mode. My body is seemingly reacting on its own. This is wild. I'm standing tall just like the time I stood in front of the Monster.

NOTHING TOUCHES MY SISTER.

The park is dead silent. Aaron Dinkle slowly rises to his feet, disoriented.

"What… what was that for, idiot?!" He barely manages to get the words out. I must have slammed him hard. The words that roll out of me are very low but very audible, "Stay away from my sister."

Aaron finally gathers himself and stands to his feet. Now I remember that he's probably a solid 2 or more years older than me since he was held back more than once. So his natural height added to the fact that he's a level above me makes him seem much larger, almost Monstrous. And for one second I flinch. That's all it takes. Aaron shoves me hard. I topple backward, over one level and down, skipping another and landing on the bottom. I manage to maneuver myself to not take one to the head, but I end up busting my shoulder pretty hard on the way down.

"I do what I want punk!" Aaron finalizes as he hops down from the bleachers. He saddles up on his bike

and rides off. Thank God his brother wasn't with him.
Matty, Randy, Bucky, Dave and half the park run to check
on me. I'm slow to rise. My shoulder feels like I've been
shot. I've never been shot, so I can't be very definitive in
that statement, but I'd imagine it's something like this.

"You okay man?!" Bucky's fast, so naturally, he's
the first there.
"My- My shoulder…" This is even more painful
than the kick to the crotch. If I wasn't surrounded by dang
near everyone on the planet right now I'd cry. I can't do
that though! Gotta be strong right? Matty hits me from the
other side with a massive hug. She clenches tight, it hurts,
but I let it happen.

"Thank you," she whispers. Her voice. She's
crying.

Crap. Now I'm crying.

"I'll be right back bro!" Bucky takes off like
lightning in the direction of my Grandparent's house.

I take a seat on the bleachers. People are being as
kind as they can, offering me bottles of water, a towel to
rest on, all kinds of things. Honestly, I'm trying to stay
conscious. I'm in a lot of pain and I might not have done a
very good job shielding my head after all. It's throbbing.

Matty sits next to me, holding me up. Randy sits
on the other side. She's taken a bottle of water on my

behalf and has opened it, ready to be of assistance. David speaks up, breaking the silence, "Pip, you are one crazy brave man."

Different voices rise up in agreement. I feel a slight smile forming on my face. What's this? Pride? And just as I feel like I can't hold my eyes open any longer, I hear one of the greatest sounds in the world: my Grandpa's truck.

Thirteen

It takes a few weeks, but I recover from a dislocated shoulder and a concussion. Word of my actions at the park spread like crazy. People that didn't pay me any attention have suddenly been very interested in me in one way or another. It's actually been kind of uncomfortable. Don't get me wrong, everyone loves a little attention from time to time, but some of the attention has been coming from people I don't really want anything to do with: the scrappers. And the Dinkles. All three of the Dinkles are now aware of my existence. According to Matty and Randy, the entire park hoopla has also been favorable for them in their grade, the one below me. Matty has always been one for popularity, but I guess this has brought things up for her a bit. Supposedly, she's the "untouchable" because her brother is "strong and brave enough" to take on a Dinkle. I'll admit I like to hear that last part. However, I don't want to "take on the Dinkles". I just want to play basketball and draw and paint.

It's been a few weeks, so things are dying down quite a bit and there is an excitement in the air that we're nearing the end of the school year.

"So Pip, now that your arm is better," Bucky stops there.

What's he want? Me to ask him to continue? Is he baiting me? It works.

"Yeah?"
"There's a basketball camp that happens every summer that the high school puts on for us middle schoolers. You should sign up!" Bucky's grinning, which means he has more to say. Why? Why does he do this?

"Okay?"
"They scout us man! They want to know what's comin' up in a few years."

That's the last thing on my mind right now. I think it shows because Bucky's enthusiasm drops. I act quick for his sake, "Oh that's awesome man!"

Honestly, I don't care. I just want to see my Mom this summer. We're supposed to be staying with her for a while during the break. I'm trying not to get my hopes up, but that's nearly impossible. Matty's super excited about it as well. She and Randy are inseparable now, so I'm sure that Randy will more than likely make an appearance with Mom sooner than later.   That's another thing that's intensified since the park incident.   Randy's all but confessed her undying love for me. I guess being a hero will do that. For now, I'll keep my head down to finish out the year and see what Summer brings.

I haven't been able to do much art the past few weeks with my shoulder being all jacked up, so I'm feeling it right now. Inspiration has been nearly knocking the door down and I'm ready to jump back in. I need to hammer out that MJ, Michael Jordan - not Michael Jackson, for Bucky. So I guess there is another upside to all this. It bought me more time to finish drawing MJ, Jordan - not Jackson.

School is school. The day is filled with work, we have pizza for lunch which is a bonus, we play basketball at lunch and then finish out the day. Matty, Randy and I have taken to walking home after school on the nice days now. We talk about all sorts of things. I find I'm a lot more open with Randy than I am with Bucky, she knows I'm a nerd. I guess I'm scared that Bucky and the guys will stop liking me if they find out that less than a year ago I was full-on wanting to be a Ghostbuster or Power Ranger when I grew up.

Deep in conversation, we don't realize that Aaron Dinkle, his older brother Dillion and one of their goon friends ride up on their bikes. They circle around us, stopping us in our tracks.

"You know I haven't forgotten about what happened," Aaron states with an angry tone.
"No one has," Randy barks back. She's not helping. I shoot her a look. I don't think she caught it though.
"No one has ever hit me before," Aaron continues.

"You want an apology or something?" Randy is laying it on thick now, and it's completely obvious that she didn't see my look, and that she has too much faith in me. I didn't "win" that fight per-se, and there is no way I can take on two Dinkles and a goon.

Matty is surprisingly quiet, he must be in her head. Aaron turns his attention to Randy and Matty.

"Maybe what I want to do is finish what I started with hero boy here, and then pick up where I left off with you." He points his nasty finger, that only God knows where it's been, at Matty. I feel it rising in me again. I slide myself over in front of Matty, so now Aaron Dinkle's booger finger (I just assume that picking his nose is probably the most hygienic thing he does with it) is pointed at my chest.

He shoves me, which forces me back into Matty. She stumbles back a few steps. I look back and see the look on her face, fear. Just like before on the bleachers, just like before with the Monster. Before the thought even crosses my mind I ball up my fist and punch Aaron so hard across the face that he crumples to the ground. Pain shoots up my arm from the blow, but I ignore it. I quickly turn to Matty and Randy.

"Run home! Now!"

By this point, we're only a couple of blocks from our Grandparent's home. Both girls immediately take flight. Aaron is moaning from the ground and Dinkle Number Two has dropped his bike and is headed my way. I'd focus on him a little more if it weren't for the fact that the goon is now riding his bike after Matty and Randy.

I pick up a piece of concrete from the road that's been chipped off from the natural wear and tear of driving on it, and I chunk it with all my might at the goon. I watch on as the piece of concrete, the size of a tennis ball at least, finds its mark and connects to the back of the goon's head. This action causes him to completely crash his bike right there on the spot. He seems lifeless at the moment, so I spin around with just enough time to take a fist to the stomach from Dillion Dinkle.

The blow takes all the breath out of my body. I double over and drop to my knees. Aaron has managed his way back up to his feet and kicks me hard in the ribs. If there were any air left, that would have depleted it. I fall to my side, gasping for air. Both Dinkle brothers proceed to start stomping me with their feet. I cover my head to shield myself from the blows. The problem is, I really need to shield my ribs. And just like so many times before, I can barely hold my consciousness. I feel myself slipping off into a blackout and I hear my Grandma's voice screaming out to the Dinkles, who immediately turn, grab their bikes and ride off.

I'm rushed to the emergency room where they look me over. The doctors and nurses are a little baffled as the beating I took only left me busted up and bruised. No broken bones, nothing severe. I have to tell you though, I feel pretty broken and severe. Oddly, and I can't explain this any better than how I'm about to, nor would I tell too many people, I felt the Voice. I felt the Voice when the Dinkles were beating me within an inch of my life. I felt that peace and that presence. So maybe once again, the Voice saved my life.

My Grandparents take me home and Mom is there waiting for me. I'm guessing Grandpa and Grandma called her. I'm overjoyed to see her, though I can't show too much enthusiasm. Breathing with a smile is about as much enthusiasm I can muster, considering my ribs. I crash on the couch after taking some meds the doctor prescribed.

I dream weird, vivid dreams. None of it makes any sense as it all keeps rapidly morphing into other dreams without finishing the last. I see people and recognize some: Matty, Randy, Bucky and David, Grandpa and Grandma, the friggin' Dinkles, and randomly Tony the Tiger, from Frosted Flakes, was there. I don't know. I blame the medication!

When I wake I'm met by Mom. She's sitting on the coffee table that sits in front of the couch.

"How you doin' baby?" she asks with such worry in her eyes.
"Feel like a million bucks," I return. I don't want her to worry.

She grins. That was the aim. That's what I wanted to see.

"So, in a couple of days, when you're ready to be up and moving around, I'm going to take you and Matty home. To stay. What do you think of that?

Fourteen

I don't know what to say. Of course, I want to go with Mom! But things are good here, I mean other than the Dinkles. Things are good with Grandpa and Grandma and with Bucky and David, and Matty has Randy. Oddly, I sort of have Randy too. I have basketball here, and art. I fix things with Grandpa. I've become a fixer! I don't want to leave that. I don't want to lose any of that.

On the other hand, I'll be with Mom. I'll be able to pick back up with Tommy and Charles and Jason. I've missed out on so much. Will I be able to jump back in? They'll just have to catch me up on Toons and all that. Strangely enough, and I'll never admit this to anyone, but I sort of miss Jeremy Leaf's loud nonsense. I mean, not a lot, but there's a little piece of me that does. It's in the furthest depths of me, but I do have to admit it's there. I miss having a crush on Emily. I do not, however, miss any part of Stupid Dog. Man, I've forgotten about some of this stuff. Having Mom here is bringing all that back.

My silence concerns Mom. "Don't you want to come home with me baby?"

"Of course I do! But, what about Grandpa and Grandma?" I ask

Where are Grandpa and Grandma? Their ever-present help in time of need isn't present! I need to hear some of Grandpa's wisdom.   I need to feel some of Grandma's comfort. What is happening on the inside of me right now? The very thing I've wanted for so long is right here, right now, and I am hesitating.

"Can you move here?" I finally ask.

"Baby, I understand you've already made friends here and started a whole new life here, but I can't move here. My job is back home. I want my babies there with me though. I promise you and Matty can come visit here as often as you want."

That comes as a huge comfort. I honestly want to find a way to mash both worlds together, like a cross-over comic, but I can't. This option is the next best thing. Mom tells us she'll be back for us in a couple of days, that she loves us, and then leaves. Grandpa helps me to my bed after Mom's departure.

"You've had a pretty active few weeks haven't ya?"

I know he's referring to the fighting. "I guess so," I respond. I know Grandpa doesn't like fighting.

"You know, I'm proud of ya kid."
"What?" He's proud of me? For fighting?
"I'm not condoning the fighting, understand that," he starts. "I'm proud of the man you're becoming. You

stood up for your sister on both accounts. You're a bigger man than most grown men for that."

"I'm scared that they'll come back," I admit.

"Don't you worry about that. Police are already involved."

"You called the police?"

"Had to file a report when we took you to the ER. Police get involved when minors are brought in in your condition."

"I don't think I want to go back home," I admit to Grandpa. Tears are beginning to well up. I miss my mom so much, but my grandparents have been everything for us. We've been lower than we have ever been and they brought us out of that.

"I understand," He says

That it? The wisest man in the world ends with that? I'm baring it all here man. I'm faced with the biggest decision of my life, and you… understand? Grandpa! You gotta do better!

"Ultimately it's your choice, son. Let me put your mind at ease though. You've always got me. You understand? You ever need me for any reason at all, just pick up the phone. It don't matter what time or what day. I'll be there. Your Mom is your Mom. She's made a lot of progress and between you and me, she may need you a little more than you need her. She's going to need someone in the house to be strong. You've proven that you're more than capable of that."

I sit quietly and take in the confidence my grandpa has in me.

"But I leave that decision up to you. Either way, you're always welcome. And either way, you'll always have a bed here. You get some rest."

He stands, pulls the blanket over my body and ruffles the hair on my head lightly.

As he leaves the room Matty enters. She's not as bubbly as usual.

"What's wrong?" I ask.

"Are we going to go live with Mom?"

"What do you want to do?" I legitimately want to know. She doesn't seem to be leaning that way.

"I don't want to leave Randy, or Grandma and Grandpa," she says as she takes a seat next to me on the bed.

"Yeah."

"But I don't want to be around the Dinkles anymore."

"Yeah."

"How are you feeling?" she asks.

"Dead," I answer with a grin.

"Don't say that!" she belts. She raises her hand to smack me but catches herself. Thank goodness!

"Thank you for saving me again." She's somber. It's rare. "If I'm away from the Dinkles, so are you."

"That's true," I reply.

There's a moment of thought as she continues, "I think we should go live with Mom then."

After the conversation, I just had with Grandpa, and now this conversation with Matty. I feel obligated, not in an unfair way, but in a responsible way, to go with Mom. Mom needs me, but Matty needs me even more. The last few weeks have proven that, and if she needs me, there is nothing in this world that can stop me from being there for her.

"Okay," I finally respond.

There's a moment as we sit in silence. In that moment I feel the presence of the Voice. With that tremendous peace, I know that everything is going to be okay. If the Voice is with me, everything is going to be more than okay.

"You want me to sing you the song?" Matty asks sweetly.

"I do."

Matty sings.

I drift off to sleep.

FIFTEEN

My argument is that we should finish out the school year here and then move back with Mom. We only have less than two months of school left. I think deep down my hesitation to move back home with Mom is that I don't know where the Monster is. The last thing Mom said about him was that "he went away." I don't know what that means to the fullest.

If I were to stay here I'd have to face the Dinkles, probably all three. Talk about being stuck between a rock and a hard place! It's stupid that it doesn't matter which I choose, impending doom is lurking. Mom thinks it's best for me to come back with her. She doesn't like the fact that I've been getting into fights.

I don't like it either, Mom, but what am I supposed to do?! Just let Aaron Dinkle force himself on my sister?! Nope. Not happenin'.

Grandpa and Grandma agree with Mom that the "physical altercations" must come to an end. Trust me when I say I don't want to fight. Trust me when I say the last thing I want to do is lay a hand on another person. I want to be the furthest thing from the Monster that I can be. I want to be more like, well, more like my Grandpa.

"You have all your things?" Mom asks.

I hold up the three bags we came with less than a year ago. We've accumulated very little since then. I've learned a lot more about life though, so I'll be leaving with that. Matty and I both are completely different people now. I hear that traumatic experiences will do that - change people.

"Toss 'em in the trunk and we'll hit the road," Mom says. "You guys are going to love the new place!"

She's excited. We all are. It's good to see her and be with her, but I can't help but want to stay. My Grandpa is the closest thing to a Dad I've ever really had. It's been so good to be with him and learn from him. It's been nice to be with Grandma and her encouragement. They've pulled things out of me that I didn't realize were there, "gifts," as they call them.

I toss the bags in the back of the trunk as Matty gives her hugs and kisses to Grandma and Grandpa. Mom's lingering at the driver's side door. It's open and the "ding" reminding us all that it is open is very present. If I weren't trying to rehearse my goodbyes in my head I'm sure I'd be irritated with it by now. Matty bounces over to the back passenger door, pops it open and jumps in. I make my way to my Grandparents. I'm moving slow. They know I am.

"Come here boy!" Grandpa grabs my arm and pulls me into their hug sandwich. Feels nice.

"I'm gonna miss you guys," I say fighting back tears.

"You can come over anytime you want. If your Mom can't drop you off we'll come get you." Grandma to the rescue! They've said that very thing about a million times over this past week, but this time - while the car is loaded and waiting to take me away - it sticks. It's comforting.

"Okay." Even though I'm still fighting tears, I feel a lot better.

"You sure you don't want to take your art stuff?" Grandma asks.

"I grabbed the pads, pens and sketching stuff. I want to leave the rest for when I come back."

"Sounds good," she says with a smile.

Grandpa guides me out in front of them, toward the car. "You take care of them, and yourself. Call me if you need me."
"I will."

He leans in a little closer to me, "Make sure you get quiet too." I know what he means. He means the quiet that was out when we were fishing. He means the quiet that comes when we're working on the truck. He means the quiet that The Voice likes to speak in. It's peaceful.

I smile. He smiles back and rubs my hair like he always does. I turn and make my way to the car. Matty's in the back, singing something to herself.   Mom is all smiles.

"Ready to rock?" she calls.
"I am…" I turn and wave at my Grandparents. I'm now at the car.
"Love you guys!" Grandma calls.
"Love you too," I answer. I turn to Mom as I open the door, "Ready to rock!"

In the past week, while Matty and I were saying our goodbyes to all of our friends at school, Mom was re-enrolling us in our old school. I will say I'm pretty excited to see Tommy, Charles and Jason again. I finished the drawing of MJ, Michael Jordan, not MJ, Michael Jackson, and I gave it to Bucky as my goodbye present. He was blown away. His reaction made me feel good about how far I've come with art. I don't plan on slowing down!

I think I'd like to make my own cartoons when I get older so kids are nerding out over my Toons like I always have over Batman, The X-Men, Spider-Man, Animaniacs and well, honestly, the list doesn't end.

The goodbye with Randy, well there really wasn't one. She vowed to track us down if she had to. Pretty sure she and Matty are going to be best friends for the rest of their lives. I hope they are. That'd be awesome for them. I drew her a picture. I had to think very hard and very carefully about what I was going to draw her so she wouldn't read between the lines that aren't really there. I didn't want her thinking that I was professing some kind of undying love. I just wanted her to know that her friendship meant something to me. I drew her a cartoon character of a BLT sandwich. She's obsessed with BLTs. That's all she ever wants to eat. I mean, I like them, but I don't view BLTs as a breakfast, lunch and dinner - all in the same day - type of food. No, that's ice cream! It really didn't matter how much thought I put into the drawing, or what I drew, she took it as the absolute that one day we will be getting married. I could have drawn her a picture of a dog taking a dump, and she still would have seen hearts somehow.

I painted a picture for Grandpa and Grandma. It's the landscape I've been working on, that includes the pond that Grandpa took me to. They liked it so much they hung it over their fireplace in the front room! Though I thought I did a pretty good job, I wouldn't say it was mantle-worthy or anything. Makes me proud to see it hanging there, though!

Secretly I've been illustrating and writing my own comic book series. It's about a dude that wakes up every day with powers that are growing, almost like every day there's a new ability. Turns out it's because his dad was this scientist that was exposed to a chemical compound.

Now it didn't affect the dad, but it was passed down to the son. The dad did end up passing away because of being exposed to the chemicals for so long, which left the mom, the son and the sister (who will be getting powers later in life - just not yet), a fortune because of the life insurance. So now he's a billionaire with increasing superpowers! I'm still working on it. I keep writing and rewriting the first draft. Once I'm comfortable with it I'll see what Matty thinks. Then maybe I'll let other people see it.

I hope that when I visit Grandpa and Grandma I'll be able to play ball with Bucky.   I don't want what happened to me, Tommy, Charles and Jason to happen to me and Bucky. I guess we'll see.

"You guys hungry?" Mom asks.
"Always!" announces Matty.
I follow up with, "I could eat."
"What you guys want? Anything! We will eat anything your little hearts desire and then we will go home and unpack!"
"Pizza!" Matty and I are in unison. If there's one thing we can agree on – well, we agree on a lot of things - but if there is one thing we can agree on… it's pizza!

"Pizza it is!"

Sixteen

It's weird being back in this town after being gone for so long. We ate at Pizza Hut, my Pizza Hut. Unfortunately, the Aphrodite of waitresses wasn't working. It didn't affect me much. Not much can when I'm in the presence of Pepperoni Pizza.

> ***Once I'm married, my wife is going to have a very difficult time because I just may want to name my first child Pepperoni. Maybe I should get a dog and name it Pepperoni to get it out of my system? But that's the problem! I don't want Pepperoni out of my system! I always want Pepperoni in my system!***

Mom's taking the scenic route seemingly as it's taking forever to get us to this new house that she's been raving about! This town isn't very big, to begin with, I mean we used to bike everywhere.

> ***Wait. BIKES!***

"Mom," I start. "Are our bikes at the new house?"

"I'm sorry hon'. We're going to have to get new bikes."

New bikes?! My bike was perfect. I had stickers all over it. There was absolutely no sign of any kind of paint job on that bad boy. It was decked out in every kind of sticker you could think of. It took a long time to get it that way. People would give me stickers just for my bike. I didn't even care what kind of sticker it was! It was awesome. I guess it's gone now. It took years to get my bike that way. All for nothing now.

"Why? What happened to our old bikes?" I ask.

"We will talk about that tomorrow. Let's just enjoy tonight. Tomorrow is Sunday. We'll get to work on your rooms and spend the day together because Monday you start school back up."

"Room-s-?" I ask.

Mom says nothing. She's all smiles.

"We have our own rooms, Mom?" Matty is throbbing in the back seat.

No response from Mom, other than a smile, as she pulls off the street into a driveway of a blue and white house. It has a front porch and a weeping willow tree in the front yard.

"This is it!" Mom exclaims. "This is home!"

The sun is nearly down, so it's not as easy to take it in to the fullest, but I like what I see so far.

She unlocks the front door and lets us in. It's a much bigger house than we're used to. This is awesome! There's not a lot of furniture, but it kind of seems like we're starting over here. At least, from what I can gather, that's what's happening. I know Mom said, "We'll talk tomorrow," but that's what it seems. So the furniture and all that good stuff will come.

"Go crazy," she says.

Both Matty and I quickly run through every square inch of the house. A Post-It note on each of our doors identify our rooms. I open the door to two windows, a couple of boxes, and a sleeping bag on the floor. My old Power Rangers sleeping bag.

I take in the space. The boxes have my name written on the side. I walk up and open one. My comics! I quickly open another, some of my toys! There aren't many more boxes, but the ones I open, hold more of the things I thought I'd lost forever. Though I know I don't have everything, it's nice to have some of the things. This day is shaping up nicely.

"Whatcha think kiddo?" Mom's voice comes from behind me. I spin around to see her standing in my doorway. I can't help but smile. She smiles back. "We'll work on getting beds and furniture and everything this week."

> *I don't care about any of that. This is good. I'm here with Mom and Matty. I'm here with things that make me… ME. No Monster and no Dinkles. This is good. It may be a clean start, but it's a good clean start.*

After a minute passes of Mom watching me rediscover so many of my treasures she comes to the realization that we haven't heard Matty make a noise for a few minutes. Never a good sign.

"Matty?" Mom calls.

I rise from my floor. And follow Mom to the other side of the hallway where Matty's room is. So cool to say. We have our own rooms! Mom knocks on the door and opens it. Matty is well underway unpacking all her boxes and organizing things according to where they will go.

"We're going to need a bookshelf right there," she informs as she points to a spot against the far wall.

"Is that so?" Mom questions playfully.

"Oh, yes ma'am!" Matty replies, matter of fact.

Mom's already unpacked the kitchen and her room, which is on the other side of the house. The bathroom is unpacked as well. Seems like Mom's been staying here for a while. So we spend the rest of the evening unpacking our things and playing games together until bedtime. Just like old times. Just Mom, Matty and me.

I'm having a hard time sleeping. The room is empty and I hear my breathing. It seems louder than it should. In fact, everything seems louder than it should.

Even the quiet is loud…

I turn to face my door, which I left open, and get an eye full of Matty hobbling in with her bedding. She nearly scares the crap out of me.

"I can't sleep," she whispers.

"Same here," I whisper back.

"Can I sleep in here with you?"

"Yeah."

She lays her blankets down next to me and plops down.

"It's really quiet here," Matty says.

"I know. We'll get used to it. We had to get used to Grandpa and Grandma's house too."

"Yeah."

"You like your room?" I ask.

"I think so. I like my stuff being in there."

"Yeah. Mom's gonna get us some beds and stuff, so everything's gonna be good."

A moment passes as we lay and listen to the crickets outside my windows. Matty sings the song and we drift off to sleep.

Seventeen

The sunlight peeking through the blinds of my window wakes me. It's Sunday. It's get-stuff-for-the-room day. It's hang-out-with-Mom day. It's get-some-answers-about-what's-been-going-on-for-the-last-several-months day. I don't want to ruin anything Mom has planned, so I'll wait and see if Mom is going to bring it all up.

Matty's snoring next to me. That girl sleeps hard. I need to find a way to sneak out of here so I don't wake her. Maybe I can get those answers first thing this morning. Kind of seems like the hesitation is Matty learning "adult things" before she should. I mean, I know I'm not an adult, but I'm ready. I was thrust into it. I'm already a perceptive person, so I tend to learn things "before I should" anyway. Matty seems not to care. If it doesn't affect her in the moment she really doesn't bother with it.

I slowly adjust myself to try and shimmy out of my sleeping bag. Why the crap did I zip it all the way up last night? I already know trying to unzip it is the wrong move. I might be able to unzip a few teeth before it starts to wake her.

If I do it like a Band-Aid and just blast through to unzip it all at once, then it'll sound like friggin' R2-D2 when he screams. I can't have that. She'll definitely wake up and I won't have the opportunity to have the one-on-one with Mom. So I'm left with the shimmy. The eternal, this-is-taking-forever, shimmy.

Finally free, I tiptoe my way out of the room. I'm going to try and close the door, but if it so much as makes one tiny squeak, I'm abandoning that mission. I try the door a little. No squeak.

Okay.

I try a little more. No squeak.

Okay! This is good.

I try a little more. Tiny squeak.

Freaking crap! I shouldn't have gambled with the door!

I stop, breathless, and wait to see if Matty is up. I can no longer see into the room since I nearly have it closed. The silence coming from the room makes me uneasy. After a few more seconds, the snoring starts back up again.

Whew! Dodged a bullet!

I turn and walk out into the living room. I can see Mom in the kitchen, it's an open floor plan. She's leaning up against the counter, holding a coffee cup with both hands lifted to her face and looking out the window. She turns as I enter the room. I quickly shoot a finger up to my mouth to inform her that silence is of the utmost importance at this very moment. She gets the point. She winks at me and nods with her head for me to come join her in the kitchen. It's not a long walk, and since there's minimal furniture in the house it's a straight shot. I hop up onto the counter across from where Mom is leaning.

"How'd you sleep?" she asks.
"Eh. Okay, I guess," I respond.
"When did Matty join you?"
"Pretty much right away."
"When did she start snoring?" she asks with a smile.
"Pretty much right away." I return the smile.

At that moment, as the comedy gods would have it, Matty barks out a thunderous snore that causes her to choke for a second. She immediately returns to the continual in-and-out rumble she was producing previously.

I have a hard time with the word previously. Not saying it or reading it or anything. It's just anytime I hear it or read it, in my head, I hear the announcer say, "Previously on The Mighty Morphin' Power Rangers." Maybe it's dumb. I don't know. No one else knows about it though. Not even Matty knows. To be fair, if she knew everyone would, so there's that.

With Matty's thunderclap snore and choke Mom and I have a hard time not laughing aloud. Our laughter would wake her without a doubt, so we cover our mouths and quietly choke on the laughs we're holding back. Holding it in makes it worse though. It makes it funnier for some reason. Then your throat starts burning and you just want to get it out, because you want to laugh! Who doesn't want to laugh? I mean even super villains laugh. It's always maniacal and in the weirdest places, like, "why is that funny to you?" They still laugh though.

Mom takes a drink of her coffee and then looks at me. She's thinking. I know because I'm a thinker, and that's what thinkers do. Things get quiet and they look at something until the right words come. Sometimes the right words don't come and that's when it gets really awkward because sometimes you're staring at a person. Then they ask you, "What?" And you don't have anything to respond with, and then they think you're weird. Yep. That's the life of a thinker.

"So we've got to get you guys some furniture," she finally says.

"Yep."

"Problem is, it's Sunday." She takes a drink of coffee. "We might be able to find a few things at Wal-Mart I guess."

Sweet. Wal-Mart. I bet I can talk her into getting me a new toy!

"We'll get ready and head out as soon as Matty's up."

"Hey Mom," I start.

"Yeah?"

I want to ask all the questions. Should I though? Is this the right time? I thought it was the perfect time earlier, but these questions seem to be hard ones. I'm sure it'll ruin the moment.

"What's up kid?"

This isn't the moment. I don't want to upset her.

"Love you."

It's like I caught her off guard or something. She seems surprised.

"Oh, I love you too."

I hop off the counter and head to my bedroom. I'm waking Matty up. I don't know what else to do. If I have to wait for the moment, and this isn't it, then I need to do something to distract myself from waiting for the moment. There's nothing I hate more than waiting. I take that back. I hate the Monster more, but waiting is a close second.

I open my door and Matty is lying face down in her pillow. I don't know how this girl survives sleeping every night. But she always defies all odds, so why would sleeping face down in a pillow be any different? I nudge her foot with mine.

"Wake up Sis!" I whisper.

Why am I whispering? I don't know. I'm quietly trying to wake her? Make sense? No, it does not.

Nevertheless, it's what I'm doing for some reason. I nudge her again and decide to abandon the whisper.

"Get up, girl."

"Why?" she moans. She flops around trying to find that comfortable spot in the floor that doesn't exist.

"We gotta go to Wal-Mart."

And just as if I was a magician doing the famous "pulling a rabbit from my top hat" routine, Matty shoots up from under her covers and runs to her room. Now you see her, now you don't. She's got to have the perfect shopping outfit, no doubt. I grab her mass of bedding, walk to her open door and throw the heap at her. It hits her as she's bent over digging through her duffle bag for clothes, and knocks her over.

"HEY!" she screams out.

I laugh as I return to my room to find some shopping clothes of my own. Really what I wear to shop in doesn't matter to me at all. I just need something that's not going to stink when I put it on. I unzip my duffle bag and right on top is a Michael Jordan shirt that Grandpa and Grandma bought me. Bucky was jealous of it, which made me want to wear it every day. I'd tease him about it all the time. Hopefully, I get to see him when I visit Grandpa and Grandma. I'm gonna miss him. I grab the t-shirt and a pair of jeans and throw them on.

Next up, my nasty morning breath. I'm surprised Mom didn't comment on the green fog coming from my mouth. Geez! I find my toothbrush and toothpaste from my bag and make my way to the bathroom, which is in between mine and Matty's bedrooms. I barely get the toothpaste onto my toothbrush before Matty comes busting in.

"My turn!" she declares triumphantly.
"I just got in here," I return. "We can brush our teeth together."
"But I have to pee!" It's obvious she does. She's doing the dance.

"Fine." I take my toothbrush into the kitchen to brush my teeth there. Matty quickly slams the door behind me. I guess she held it as long as she could.

Mom's still at the counter as I left her. She's in think mode. I step up and brush my teeth. You're supposed to recite the Alphabet song as you brush the top, and then again for the bottom, and then again when you brush across. I find that irritating, but I'm also told that if you don't take care of your teeth that they will all fall out. I know this to be true because I have a second cousin (or something like that) who always ate candy all the time - like all the time - and all of his teeth fell out. Well, I guess the dentist pulled them out, but anyway, he's not even an adult and he has dentures. So... I sing the Alphabet song three times when I brush.

"Wow, you got ready fast!"
"Yep," I return as I wash the paste from my toothbrush and mouth.
"Guess I better get to it," she says as she reaches around me to place her empty coffee cup in the sink.

I wonder how long it's been empty. Wonder how long she's been up and what she's been thinking about.

"Mom," I turn to her.
"Yeah?" She asks.
"Are we going to talk today?"

The look on her face tells me she completely understands what I'm talking about.

Good. This may not be the moment, but I know there IS a moment that's coming soon. Good. I'm good with that.

EIGHTEEN

Wal-Mart was a smash hit. We ended up finding futon beds there. Who knew? They are metal frames, so they are super cool. I've never seen a metal bed frame before. Only wood. My frame is black and Matty's is white. We, "Made out like bandits," as Mom always says. That just means we got a lot of stuff. Matty picked out pink bedding. She's sticking to the Pink Ranger theme. Or maybe princess? I guess her favorite color really could be pink. I opted for blue and black. Mom was a little shocked at first that I didn't spring for the Jurassic Park themed bedding. I guess I'm growing up.

After the shopping spree, we got lunch at a sandwich shop that one of Mom's friends, Shari, owns. It was good to see her. It's been forever, but something was weird. Not for me or Matty, but between Mom and Shari. I assume the thanks goes to the Monster.

Now here I am, getting royally chafed at the fact that I can't get the fitted sheet to stay on my brand new mattress.   I must have turned this stinkin' thing one hundred-eighty-two thousand times. There's no rhyme or reason!

I can't bring myself to ask for help though. My pride won't let me.

"You need some help?" Mom's voice comes from the doorway behind me.

I slump in defeat. "Yes please."

Mom steps in and grabs the end that keeps popping off. She gives it a firm pull and then it's clear that I've rotated the sheet the wrong way. Again.

"Just have the sheet the wrong way is all." She informs confidently as she yanks my hard work right off the mattress.

My eyes go wide. Clearly, Mom sees the utter shock on my face that she'd just unraveled years - okay not years - but precious, precious, very, very long – almost eternal - minutes of my life that I'll never get back. And because my short-fuse is hilarious to her, she lets out a laugh as she begins stretching. At first, I watch her disgruntled, but I can't stay upset with her.

"You wouldn't have been able to figure it out so fast if I hadn't already been working on it you know," I inform her playfully.

"Oh for sure," she returns with a smile and a wink.

So now my fitted sheet *actually* fits. They should put in the directions that it takes one hundred-eighty-THREE thousand attempts before success is achieved. Or maybe not to try if you're a 12-year-old kid that's in 6th grade when you should really be in 7th grade, with zero patience for this kind of crap and you have a sister by the name of Matty. That's more like it. Way more specific and I would clearly have known that my chances of successfully making my bed were zero.

"So you're all set with your bed kiddo!" Mom tosses my comforter in the air while holding onto the bottom two corners. The top two corners land perfectly at the head of my bed and she smooths out the bottom two after the perfect landing.

Any time I try that the comforter janks to the side. Either my mom is a bed-making wizard or there is something terribly wrong with me. I hope she's a wizard. I toss my pillow onto the bed and that's that. My new bed is made with my new bedding.

"Looks like a teenager's bed," Mom says. She nudges me with her elbow. "Stop growing up so fast."

"Would if I could!" I mean it. I've seen what adults have to deal with and I'd rather be a kid for as long as I can.

Mom takes a seat on my bed and pats next to her for me to sit. I do.

"So. I promised you we'd talk."

Mom continues, "I figure we can fill Matty in when she actually wants to know."

"Okay." I'm ready. Let's do this. Let's talk.
"So go ahead."
"Huh?"

Go ahead? Go ahead and what?

Ask the questions? I figured us talking would be more her talking because I'm completely clueless of what's really been happening for the past few months.

"Ask anything. I know there are a lot of questions."

There are a lot of questions, but right here and right now... I'm blank. I wasn't expecting the 'ole switcheroo. She turned the tables on me and I wasn't ready.

Come on brain. There's a list in there somewhere.

"I uh…"   Okay.   We're formulating here. "Why?" I fumble.

Mom smiles graciously. "Okay. I'll start. Chris turned out to be a bad man." Tears well up in my eyes.

FOR THE LOVE OF BRUCE WAYNE! CONTROL YOURSELF, MAN! WHAT IS WRONG WITH YOU?!

My tears start a chain reaction in Mom. She tears up as well. She fights through, and I appreciate it.

"I'm going to make this as to the point as I can okay?"
I nod.

"Okay.   Chris hurt you.   Chris hurt me. Physically.   I know we both know and understand that. Chris wasn't like that in the beginning though, and if I'd have known this was going to happen, sweetheart…" Mom swallows hard.   She's fighting the emotions and the memories. I wipe my eyes, take in a deep breath and sit up tall. I need to be strong for her. "If I'd known, none of this would have ever happened."

A moment passes between us. Mom knows she has to share more, more of what I don't know to ask. She knows I know, yet don't know. She takes in a deep breath and lets it out slowly.

"I know that you've noticed some of your things missing. He sold all of our stuff. I was able to track down a lot of it, but not all of it. Some of it I had to prove was ours in order to get back. Some of it is just plain gone, and I'm so sorry. I will replace what I can."
"I don't care about the stuff Mom," I cut in. "I mean, I'll miss not having it and hope maybe I can get it back or whatever. But I just care about us."

Mom takes in my statement. She nods and wipes her eyes.
"Come here," she says finally as she pulls me in for a huge hug. "You're such a strong kid. Not even really a kid anymore are you? I love you my soon-to-be little man." She lets loose of the hug and stands to her feet.

"I love you too Mom."

I watch as she leaves my room. I hear her knock on Matty's door and Matty call out from inside. I listen as Mom goes in and closes the door behind her. She'll be having some form of "talk" with Matty now. Well, that was good. I don't know if all my questions have been answered, I mean... I know they haven't, but I'm satisfied for the moment. I'm sure there will probably be more "talks" in the near future. For now, I'm good. I think Mom's good too. I'll make a one-million-dollar bet that Matty is good as well.

So this is it, "The fresh start." Tomorrow, bright and early, I start back to school. My new school is my old school. I can't wait to see Tommy, Jason and Charles! I haven't had the opportunity to call them. They don't even know I'm back! This is going to be awesome!

Morning comes and I'm up with the sun. Nothing will stop me from being ready to see my best friends again! We can pick up where we left off! They'll have to catch me up on everything I missed, but I'll fall right in. This is my team, my gang, my crew. Mom drops us off.

Unfortunately, I have to finish the school year in a different class. I'm in Mr. Brown's class now. His mustache covers his entire mouth. It's obvious when he's talking because you can hear him, but if he was whispering I'm not sure anyone would know he was talking. Some say he doesn't even have a mouth. No lips!

I wonder if Mr. Brown's mustache blows in the breeze.   I

wonder if he flips it like supermodels do in shampoo commercials. Does he realize how massive it is? I wonder how much of his food gets stuck in there? This is more than a mustache. This is becoming a Wonder of the World.

Everyone step right up!

If you look here you'll see The Egyptian Pyramids! No, no one is quite sure how they were built! Over here we have The Great Wall of China! And if you look now you'll see the most elusive, the rarest of wonders... MR. BROWN'S MUSTACHE!!!

The bell rings, pulling me from my tour of the Wonders of the World. I really should have been paying attention. No time to dwell on it though! This is the bell I've been waiting on! This is the lunch bell! Here I come guys!

"Okay class, line up single file," Mr. Brown deadpans.

We quickly fall in place. We're all ready. Some more than others, but we're all ready nonetheless. Mr. Brown opens the door and we quickly shuffle out of the room and head to the lunchroom. I immediately begin my scan from left to right, right to left.

I gotta find my people!

There's Charles! He doesn't see me. The energy level on the inside of me is unreal right now. I feel like I'm vibrating. I'm going to try and surprise the guys and just sit down by them after I grab my tray of food. Today is pizza day, so I'm coming out on top clear across the board right now! The little square pizzas aren't any better than a microwave pizza, but having it at school sort of ups the value. And they always serve green beans with the pizza, which has never really made any sense to me. Why green beans? I guess no real veggie sits alongside a slice of pizza and looks at home. Maybe an entire salad? I don't know. Green beans are fine. And of course, the cherry on top, the chocolate chip cookie that comes with this arrangement. So good. I could plow through a hundred of these bad boys! The drink of choice with this lineup is a no-brainer: Chocolate milk.

I grab my tray and make my way to Charles. Jason is seated across from him. Man, I can't wait to see their faces. Tommy's probably still in line, so he'll just have to be shocked when he joins us. Too bad. He's the one I want to surprise the most. I set my tray down next to Charles and then plop down.

"Hey guys!" I beam.

My presence takes Jason by surprise so hard that he quotes Elvis, which is his surprise mechanism.

"Viva Las Vegas!" Jason exclaims.
"You're back?!" Charles blurts out simultaneously.
"Yeah, guys! I'm back! I missed you guys so much!"
"Yeah, dude! Really good to see you!" Jason returns. He's gathered himself and is out of Elvis mode now. It's for the best. Sometimes he gets stuck there and it gets real old real fast.
"So where's Tommy?" I ask.
"You don't know?" asks Charles.
"Know what?"
"Tommy moved to Indiana," Jason informs me.

The blood drains from my face.

> ***He was supposed to be here.***
> ***I was supposed to come back and pick up where we left off. Things were supposed to go back to normal; the gang, the guys, the crew, the team.***

"You, uh, you guys have his, uh, phone number or anything?" I barely get it out.
"No man. His mom kinda up and moved 'em like what happened to you," says Charles. "Except we got to say goodbye to Tommy."

This is the worst news I've ever heard. With moving to my Grandparent's house I at least knew that the guys were here and that I could reach them. There's no way to reach Tommy! My best friend of, well since I can remember, is completely gone.

"Yeah," starts Jason. "It sucks, but you're back now bro! We can hang out again!"

I nod my head in response and force a smile for the sake of Jason and Charles. Don't get me wrong, I love being back with them. It's just not the same. Tommy is gone. Tommy is completely gone. No way of finding him. My best friend is gone.

I fight the intense urge to cry. It's in my throat and feels like a burning ball of fire. I quickly lower my head and cram some pizza into my mouth. I can't let them see my face right now.

Jason starts filling me in on some of the things I've missed. I'm in and out, though I'm trying my hardest to pay attention. I want to know what I missed, but I just had a bomb dropped on me that hit me directly in the heart.

The bell rings for recess and I excuse myself to the restroom right after assuring Jason and Charles that I'll meet them on the playground. I rush in and check the stalls. I can't have anyone bear witness to the mess I'm about to become. I step to the sink and turn it on so I can wash my flushed face. The moment I see myself I can no longer hold back the waterworks. My eyes flood with water and I sob to myself there in the bathroom all alone. My heart aches. The last several months of my life have been the hardest yet. It has to get better.

"Please," I whisper. "Please help me." The feeling I get when the Voice speaks to me fills the air, and I feel at peace.

Nineteen

The next few weeks blow by, as they do when summer break is near. I fall back in with Charles and Jason. We have a lot of fun, but it's just plain different. We don't quite do what we used to. We find ourselves playing video games and reading comics a lot, not that that's any different than the days of old, but we've omitted 'toons and toys, for the most part. Matty hasn't really shown any interest in falling back in with the guys. She'll hang out with us every once in a while, but she usually jets home as soon as possible after school so she can get on the phone with Randy.

Every other weekend we go to Grandpa and Grandma's house. I've been working on a painting to express my frustrations with this past year. I can't tell if it's even turning out. It'll probably be a massive canvass of crap, but it sure is helping me feel better. And of course, we see Randy when we are there. Randy is Randy! She hasn't changed a bit. That's a good thing.

I see Bucky and Dave and some of the other guys when they are available. We play ball. They fill me in on everything that's going on with school and sports and stuff. They stay pretty busy closing out the year with track and field. Not missing anything there! I'm not the track and field type. Bucky is an every sport type though, so naturally, he goes out for everything he can. Bucky tells me that Aaron Dinkle hasn't been at school since my last little run-in with him. According to Bucky, no one knows what happened to him. His brother is still stomping around town, but Aaron has vanished. Makes me wonder. But then again, I don't want to spend much brain power on a Dinkle. Bucky says there are all kinds of rumors floating around about Aaron, and even about me. One of them is something like, I killed Aaron in battle and then went on the run so I wouldn't go to prison! Crazy talk! There are others, but they aren't quite as outrageous.

Things are feeling good. Spring always brings a level of excitement, and of course, the growing enthusiasm for summer doesn't die off until you are in the middle of it and realize you are only weeks away from school starting back up again. My favorite part of spring/early summer is this weekend. It's my birthday! Here's the real kicker, I'm having two parties! Mom is throwing me a party Friday night. I'm having Charles and Jason over and we're going to rent some movies, pig out on pizza and ice cream cake, and stay up late playing video games! It's going to be totally awesome! Then the next day Mom is taking us to Grandpa and Grandma's house and they're throwing me a party! Bucky, Dave, and Randy will be there. It's going to be a blast! I can't wait. But that's the thing about saying, "I can't wait." You really can, and you really have to. Lame.

RING!

I rush out to the car lane. No bus today! Mom is picking us up, me, Matty, Jason and Charles! We're partying all day and night baby! I clear the doors and exit into the great outdoors. The sun seems warmer, the flowers seem prettier. The annoying kids waiting in line for the busses seem less annoying. I step up to the sidewalk where Matty is already waiting.

"You excited?" she asks.

"Heck yeah I am!" I return.

"What do you think Mom got you?" she asks with a massive smile.

"You know don't you!"

"I'm saying nothing!" Her smile grows wider.

"Matty! You can't do me like that!"

"Watch me!"

"Torture!"

Matty and I share a laugh as Charles and Jason step up. They have sleeping bags and an extra duffle bag each.

"Dude. I'm stoked!" beams Jason.

"Don't say anything man!" Charles barks.

"What?!" returns Jason. "Dude. All I said was I was stoked!"

"You were about to tell him! I could sense it!" Charles is on edge. Come to think of it, Charles was acting weird at lunch and recess today too.

"You need to take a chill pill. I was thinking about the pizza and ice cream cake," explains Jason.

"No! No! Man! I could feel it! You were about to tell him!"

"Tell me what?" I demand. They are acting very, very weird.

"Chuck here," starts Jason.

WHOA! Jason NEVER calls Charles Chuck! That's a me thing, and I only do it when I'm max irritated! Jason just pulled the Chuck card, so that means something is up.

Jason continues, "Thinks I was about to tell you about your present."

"DUDE!" Charles explodes.

"I didn't say anything!" Jason is all worked up now. His voice is rising.

"Guys," I cut in. "What present?"

Are they talking about their presents or Mom's present?

"I told em," Matty says with a mischievous grin.

It's Mom's present!

"You guys know what my mom got me?!" I need to calm down. I'm nearly yelling.

"I can't take this pressure!" Chuck looks as if he's going to have a heart attack. "Matty, you know I'm terrible with secrets!"

Matty is grinning from ear to ear. If she had popcorn she'd be shoveling it into her mouth. Jason pats Charles on the back as he's now bent over with his hands on his knees. This sight is hysterical. And just like that, like the breath of fresh air Charles needs, Mom pulls up and bails them out. I can't very well grill them for their knowledge if she's around.

"Oh thank God!" Charles cries as he runs to the car. Jason, Matty and I follow. Mom has me take the passenger seat, being that I'm the birthday boy. I'm more than happy to do so. As soon as we're in, Matty leans up between the seats. "Hey, Mom! Charles was just telling us a hilarious story! You should hear it!"

"Okay! Let's hear it, Charles!" Mom adjusts the rearview mirror to better see the backseat. I think I can literally hear all the air leave Charles' lungs. His eyes are going to pop out of his head. There is the most awkward silence right now. Even more awkward than the time in Transitional One Class - that class I was forced to take because of my "attention span" - that Frank, I forgot his last name, asked to go to the bathroom. The teacher didn't let him because we had already gone to the bathroom. So Frank straight up pooped his pants, right there in class. It was bad. It was awkward. I felt so bad for him. This is feeling more awkward than that. Come to think of it, there's no way this is more awkward than that. Unless Charles starts pooping himself.

Matty bursts out in laughter, nearly scaring us all to death. There's the Matty we all know and love! I miss her. Since we've moved back she's sort of stopped with all things me. She's not being mean or anything. She's just been spending her time at school with other girls and at home, she's usually on the phone with Randy. Mom takes Matty's outburst of laughter as Matty pulling a prank and she starts laughing. With Matty and Mom laughing, I have no chance. Plus seeing Charles squirm, nearly to death, is hilarious! Jason follows suit and starts laughing and then finally Charles after he swallows his stomach.

We pull into the house, charged and ready to go. Mom barely gets the car parked before we are out and at the front door. She's all smiles. She loves seeing us this happy. Matty is acting as she used to. She's joking around with Charles and Jason. We keep trading insults and even Mom jumps in with a ton of "your Mom" insults. We don't even know how to respond! She's our Mom!

The pizza is delivered. Mom went overboard and bought 3XL pizzas! All pepperoni, baby! We sit in front of the TV and watch The Fresh Prince of Bel-Air. Love this show!

"Okay," Mom says as she turns to me. "I think we need to do the ice cream cake first, and then we will do presents. So you guys come to the kitchen and we'll cut the cake." Every time I hear someone start a sentence with "Cut the…" I always think it's going to end with "cheese". It never does, but I always want it to. I mean, cut the cheese means to fart. Who doesn't love fart, butt and poop humor?

Mom pulls the cake from the freezer, the glorious chocolaty goodness. She opens it up and sets it on the table. It's a white frozen frosting with a crazy tie-dye looking design on it. My name and Happy 13th B-day are spelled out in the white space that's not taken up by the design. Mom starts singing Happy Birthday and everyone joins in. This is the greatest. This is making the dark spots of the past few months seem a little less dark.

I do wish Tommy was here, but I have Matty back. Even if things go back to the way they were tomorrow, at least I have right now. I have Mom and Charles and Jason, and I have ICE CREAM CAKE!

Mom *cuts the cake* and we eat around the table in the kitchen. We're all laughing and having a good time. I overeat. I had already decided in my heart earlier that day that I was going to eat as much pizza and as much ice cream cake as I could possibly hold down. I know the line of too much and then throwing it all up because it was too much. I stop right up against that line.

"Okay, guys!" Mom exclaims as she takes our plates. "It's present time!"

I'm so excited. I can barely contain myself.

"I'll be right back," informs Jason as he rises from his chair.
"Me too," states Charles.

They both exit into the living room and reappear moments later with wrapped gifts. They're all crumpled up because they were in their duffle bags, but I don't care one bit! I'm going to rip that paper off like it's life or death.

"You go ahead and open these gifts and I'll be right back," Mom says. She disappears around the corner into her room. Matty is bouncing up and down. She knows. I know she knows and she knows I know she knows. She's way too entertained with all of it. Charles tosses his present to me.

"Open it," he says.
"Oh, you want me to open this?" I hold up his present in sarcasm.
"Yeah, dummy! Just open it!" He chuckles.

I rip into it. It's a Jurassic Park Dilophosaurus toy, like the one that eats Dennis in the movie!

"Awesome!" I exclaim.

"You can make the throat mane thing pop out! Just like in the movie!" Charles is pointing at the box as I'm holding it up.

I have the T-Rex, a Velociraptor, a Brachiosaurus and several of the people. This is a great addition to my collection! I just might have to get a bookshelf and display them all. Well, then I'd want to display all of my toys and I have so many. I'll think this through later.

Jason slides his present across the table.

"Looks like a stack of comics," I inform. "Is it comics?"
"Just open it, dude!"

I slowly begin the opening process. I don't want to damage or, dog ear, the comic books, so I'm taking a little more time on this go-round. I'm pretty particular with my comics looking absolutely clean and un-creased. I believe they call it "mint condition." I finally get the wrapping paper off. It's a stack, Books 1-6, of the Jurassic Park comic that's recently been released.

"Wow! So cool!" I examine the cover of each book. I'm looking forward to reading these.

Mom reappears with a massive box and a smaller box on top of it. Matty is jumping up and down, she can barely contain herself.

"Okay my teenager," she starts. "I wanted to get you something super special this year."

Matty, Charles and Jason are all beaming, vibrating even. They are all in on my big present, and they all managed to keep it quiet. I'm impressed! Matty nearly shouts as I reach for the big box, "The small one first! I helped with it!"

I redirect my aim and reach for the smaller box. Matty is emitting this high-pitched noise that would throw dogs into a frenzy. Good! Maybe Stupid Dog can hear it, even though we are clear across town now. I can't help but smile at her craziness. I rip into the wrapping paper, which is Jurassic Park themed.

Wait, everything has been Jurassic Park so far…

"HOLY CRAP!" I scream. "This is the Jurassic Park game for Sega Genesis!" I'm in awe. "But wait," I look to Mom. "I don't have a Sega."

She pushes the big box toward me with her big beautiful smile spread across her face. My mouth drops open and my eyes go wide.

Matty starts clapping and chanting, "OP-EN IT! OP-EN IT!" Charles and Jason join in. I can't help it. I rip into that box like I'm a bulldog and it's a slab of steak. I'm ravenous. I wouldn't be surprised if I have to wipe slobber and drool from my mouth when all this is said and done. I finally get all the paper off and there it is in all its wonderful glory.

"Ladies and Gentlemen," I say in a hushed tone. "I give you… THE SEGA GENESIS!" The last part comes out a lot less hushed. I'm beside myself. Mom is cracking up at how odd I'm acting. It's all the sugar in my system plus the adrenaline rush from getting the worlds' greatest gaming console AND the friggin' Jurassic Park game to play on it! I throw my arms around Mom, nearly knocking her back.

"Oh!" she exclaims as she puts her arms around me. I squeeze hard. She squeezes back.

"Thank you Mom! I love you!"
"You bet kiddo. I love you too."

Naturally, we stay up way too late taking turns playing Sega. The cool thing is, the console came with Sonic the Hedgehog! I have Sonic and Jurassic Park! I don't remember turning the Sega and TV off that night. We just fall asleep. It must have been Mom. What a great night! What a great birthday!

TWENTY

Charles wakes me, "Hey man, my Mom is on her way to get me."

I'm in a daze. I can't feel my arm. I must have been sleeping on it or something.   That tingly painful feeling that hurts when you don't move it, but hurts when you do. You don't want to move it because you know it'll suck when you do, but you know you have to in order to speed up the process. At least it's not one of my legs. That happens to me all the time when I spend too much time reading comics on the toilet. It sucks.

"What time is it?" I ask as I sit up.
"I think it's almost eleven," Charles replies as he rolls up his sleeping bag.
"Dang! Eleven!"
"Who is?" Jason sits up, even more dazed than I was mere seconds ago.
"Who is what?" Charles asks with a smile.

It's clear Jason is snapping out of a dream, so who knows what he's actually asking us right now.

"Huh?" Jason asks, throwing himself into further confusion.

Charles and I share a laugh at Jason's expense.

Where's Matty?   She would have eaten this up!

I crawl from my sleeping bag as Jason rubs the sleep from his eyes. Mom enters the room. "Okay, boys. Time to get up and get around. Charles, your Mom will be here any minute, and I just got off the phone with your Mom, Jason. She'll be here shortly."

Jason nods through a yawn. I roll up my sleeping bag and tie it up.   Charles has all his things ready and sitting by the door. Jason is slow to move, but he's getting there. He may not even realize he's awake at the moment.

"Geez!   Sleep all day why don't you!" Matty chuckles as she enters the room.

"Where've you been?" I ask.

"Me and Mom have been having a girl's morning," she informs.

"What the heck is a girl's morning?" I ask.

Matty smiles, "Just girls, doing what girls do. In the morning."

"What do girls do in the morning?" Charles asks.

"My mom takes like two hours to do her hair in the morning," Jason cuts in.

"His first actual sentence! Welcome to the party buddy!" I prod with a smile.

Mom enters the room again, she's zipping all over the house this morning. It's clear she's rested and that we stayed up way too late. I have to quiz her before she exits the room again. I'll get to the bottom of what a "Girl's Morning" is right now!

"Hey, Mom!" I call.
"Yep?" she stops momentarily.
"What'd you and Matty do this morning?" I ask confidently. I've got this.
"Oh you know," she replies. "Girl stuff." Then she leaves the room.
Matty is all smiles.

"What the crap is Girl Stuff?!" I'm flustered. It wouldn't be a big deal, except Matty is acting as if we -boys- have really missed out on something! There's a knock at the door. Charles opens it up and his mom is there. Charles calls out as he grabs his things, "Hey thanks for letting me stay the night!"

Mom pops her head back in, "You bet!' Mom waves at Mrs. Hughes and she waves back at Mom. I hear Mrs. Hughes call, "Happy birthday" to me as the door closes. The whole exchange ends in less than two minutes. I would have said, "Thank you", but they were gone before I could even think. I'm a tad slow this morning. Nearly the exact same thing happens with Jason and his mom, except Jason's mom is a bit of a talker. Mom had to shoot the breeze for a few extra minutes.

I personally don't remember what time we're supposed to head to Grandpa and Grandma's house, just sometime after lunch, but being that it's eleven, lunch is upon us. I take my things to my room and decide that a shower is going to be for the best. Not only do I sort of smell, I also need to wake up. I'm still pretty groggy. I have no clue how late we stayed up, nor any clue as to how much sleep we got. Too late, not enough. We'll run with that.

Shower, lunch, car, the road. The turn of events move faster than my mind. I really should have thought through on staying up as late as we did. I do have to say that a big part of me thinks it's worth it. That Jurassic Park game is so unbelievably fun. And there are times playing it that it's just as jumpy as the movie! Plus getting to hang out like that with Matty and Charles and Jason. So much fun.

We pull into the driveway at Grandpa and Grandma's house. They have blue and white and black helium balloons tied to their mailbox. They're swaying and tangling lightly in the spring breeze. There's one lone balloon that's bigger and floats taller than the others. It's shiny and has the words, "Happy Birthday" across it. It's glimmering in the sun. Definitely an attention grabber. Everyone on the block knows for sure that it's someone's birthday. Here comes round two! Should have paced myself a little.

"Here we are! Party number two for the teenager!" Mom grins as she elbows me. She's really enjoying this me becoming a teen thing. She just keeps saying it over and over. "Here comes the teenager," "Teenager this," "Teenager that," "Teenager in the house!" Yes. She does say that. And yes, it is embarrassing. She's Mom though, so I let it slide. I don't know how much more I'll be able to take, but for now, I'll let her have it.

Mom parks the car and we all jump out. Matty sprints ahead and blasts through the front door before I can even get to the porch. I like Grandpa and Grandma's front porch. They have a bench style porch swing that's bolted to the ceiling. Lots of nights spent out there thinking and questioning. All the deep, inside stuff, you know?

Mom hurries me along. I'm in my head and I guess I tend to move slower when that happens. She puts her arm around my shoulder and walks beside me, which naturally forces my stride to quicken. I look at her and she at me. I'm eye to eye with her now. Guess I hit a growth spurt. She smiles her beautiful smile, which always forces me to return with a smile of my own. I guarantee my smile holds nothing in comparison to hers, yet I still do. I smile back every time.

Two steps up and we're on the porch. Mom opens the door for me, "Get in there Birthday Boy!"

I step in and am immediately met by not only the amazing smell of Grandma's baking, singing too! Grandpa, Grandma, Randy, Matty all walk in, and Mom closes the front glass door behind her.

"Happy Birthday to yoooooooou!!!" They all belt out in unison. I hide a grin. I don't know why, but I'm embarrassed. I like attention fine enough, but a ton of people looking at you and singing at you, not just to you, at you. It's a little weird.

Grandma outdid herself. She baked the cake, made a pie, made these amazing little chocolate candies that have peanuts inside. I can literally make myself sick off of them, so I make her ration them. She can't tell me how many she actually made because I have zero self-control when it comes to those candies. Peanut Clusters, that's what she calls them. And then she's promised my favorite dinner as well! I won't be able to walk. I won't be able to move. I may not even have room to breathe.

We all have cake and ice cream. We sit around the kitchen table and talk and laugh. Bucky and Dave and none of the other guys could make it due to an early basketball camp. When I first found this out I was a little bummed, but this is good. This is all I need. I'm sure I'll catch up with all the guys soon enough.

We all move to the living room for presents. The location change is absolutely necessary. I'm starting to hear the Peanut Clusters call my name. I need to put some distance between me and them now or it could all be over.

"I got you something," Randy says as she sets a gift bag in front of me on the coffee table. I look her in the eye as she takes a step back. There's no smile or ornery grin on her face. I look at Matty. She'd crack. If this was a prank I'd see it on her face. But nothing, no grin or smile or smirk from either of them. I look at the blue and black striped gift bag with black tissue paper poking out the top. I grab the bag with both hands and bring it to my lap.

It's not heavy. Wonder what it could be?

I pull out some of the tissue paper, and then more. There's quite a bit of it. Finally, I reach down into the bag and I find something of rough cloth. Feels like a basketball jersey, I think to myself. I pull out the bag's contents and I can barely believe what I see. I'm holding a Shaquille O'Neal jersey! The blue and white, Orlando Magic, number 32, Shaq jersey!

You see, I like MJ, yes, both Michael Jackson and Michael Jordan, and I like Scottie Pippen. A lot of that is because that's also what Bucky calls me, but I really like Shaq! I liked Shaq even when I barely kept up with basketball, and even more so now! Randy got me a Shaq jersey for my birthday!

"I saved up my allowance for like, forever, so I could get it. You like it?" she asks with concern in her voice.

I've lingered too long in my head again. The shock has to wear off! I have to respond!

"You can exchange it if you want." There's a heavy level of disappointment in her voice. "I just thought that -"

"Yes!" I nearly yell, interrupting her. My awkward outburst startles everyone. "I mean, sorry, yes. I love it!" I catch the look on Randy's face as it changes from disappointment to complete joy. I think she's happier than I am, which is crazy because... I HAVE A SHAQ JERSEY!

"You'll have to step outside to see what your Grandma and I got you," Grandpa informs as he stands to his feet.

Everyone stands to their feet and Grandpa motions for us all to follow him out the back door. I slide the jersey on over the top of my t-shirt. Perfect fit.

"Thank you!" I smile at Randy.
"You're welcome," she blushes back.

We all file back through the kitchen behind Grandpa, where I'm reminded of all the food that will be meeting its match later. After the kitchen, we move through the utility room and out the back door onto the back porch. I have zero clue as to what could be back here. We're mere steps from Grandpa's shed, and off to the right in the backyard is the storm cellar, so there's that. Grandpa steps off the porch and as he does I get an eye-full of what Grandpa and Grandma got me.

"YOU GOT ME A BASKETBALL GOAL?!"

Grandpa laughs. I'm beside myself. I make my way to the goal, which has a basketball sitting next to it. This could be the best birthday(s) I've ever had! Last night plus today, there is absolutely no comparison! I'm calling it. My 13th year is going to be my best year ever!

Twenty One

Over the next few weeks, we start spending more and more time at Grandpa and Grandma's house. The school year comes to an end and we start spending time there through the week, not just weekends here and there. That helps Mom out a lot since she still has to work. Must be lame knowing your kids are having a great time being out of school when you still have to go to work every day.

The time at Grandpa and Grandma's is well spent on art, basketball and being with Matty again. Of course, being with Matty also means being with Randy. That's no big deal though! I don't mind it at all. Matty's time is usually spent with Randy or on music. They both do spend quite a bit of time watching me in the garage, but even that time is filled with their plans of world domination in the music biz.

Summer is well underway and we're hanging out on the regular with Bucky, Dave and every once in a while someone else will join us. We're actually all becoming really good friends; Bucky, Dave, Randy, Matty and myself. We play ball of course, but we find ourselves just listening to music and talking, doing nothing in particular. When we're home with Mom, there's still Jason and Charles! Matty even jumps in with us from time to time now. That Sega is getting plenty of attention! Staying with

Mom is great and we're even starting to see some of her old friends come back around from time to time. It's not like it once was, but it's been good seeing them. They of course do what all adults do when they haven't seen kids in a while, "You've grown so much! You're getting so big! What has your Mom been feeding you two?" All the dumb stuff that you have to react to as a kid.

Matty and I are getting close again. It was getting tough there for a while. I don't like feeling distance between us. I don't know. I guess I like to think that when I don't have anyone, I'm never alone. I have Matty. But there for a little while, it felt as if that wasn't the case. I know I'm the oldest sibling, so maybe I shouldn't be as dependent on her when it comes to my peace of mind. Maybe.

I'm sitting in, watching and sketching, as Matty's taking a piano lesson from Grandma. She's getting really good. Grandma is a good teacher, so that helps in addition to Matty's natural talent. She's come a long way from Mary Had A Little Lamb.   I'm drawing a picture of them together. Not to toot my own horn, but I'm getting pretty good at drawing. My people actually look like the people they're supposed to. I have a ways to go, but I'm starting to take a lot of pride in my work.

That's a weird saying. "Not to toot my own horn." Who says toot? Toot means fart! Why wouldn't I toot my own horn? I wouldn't want anyone else blowing their slobber into an instrument I'm supposed to be blowing into. That's nasty. I realize it's supposed to be like saying, "not to brag," but it's such a weird way to say it. I've heard my Grandpa say it before, that's probably why I said it. Why not toot your own horn, though? I mean, if you're good at tooting, shouldn't you toot it? I've said toot like a hundred times now and honestly if I'd have been saying it out loud I'd probably already have busted out laughing. Matty definitely would have.

"Great job today kiddo!" Grandma says as she stands to her feet.

"Thanks Grandma!" Matty keeps tinkering with the keys.

"I'm going to go start on dinner," Grandma announces to the two of us as she takes her leave.

"What you drawing?" Matty shoots over her shoulder as she plays a few chords in a pattern.

"It's a secret," I say with a grin.

"No it isn't," she pops as she tosses a look my way.

"It is, and you can't see what it is until I'm finished with it," I inform her.

Matty stops playing and turns to me. "That's not fair! You should have just said you were drawing a fish or something!"

"I'm not drawing a fish though!" My grin widens.

·   "Well when are you going to be finished with it then?" she demands.

"I'm done."

"You're so dumb! Let me see!" she says with a grin.

She gets up from the piano bench and sits next to me on the couch that's seated against the wall across from the piano. I show her the drawing of her and Grandma together. It's from my view, so their backs and the back of their heads are the most visible.

"Awe! It's me and Grandma!" She nudges me with her elbow like Mom always does . She grins at me and then informs me, "I'm keeping it." She grabs the sketch paper and bounces off to the bedroom.

A knock at the front door distracts me from protesting her thievery. I get up to answer the door. The front door is almost always open, but that's because there is a glass door that stays closed and serves as the front door for the most part. Grandpa and Grandma call it the screen door, but it's not made of screen. It's made of glass. No one argues that point with them though, so it's called the screen door.

I can easily see who is on the other side of the door. Bucky is standing there obviously trying not to be rude and peer into the house. I can see how that would be difficult. I don't know a lot of people with glass "screen doors", so I don't really have a problem with accidentally eavesdropping with my eyes when knocking on someone's door. Anyway, Bucky's standing there with his basketball as I open the door.

"Hey Pip! You wanna go play at the park? Bunch of us getting together!" His enthusiasm shows in his eyebrows bouncing up and down at a rapid pace. As if the faster he moves them the more convincing he is. I mean, it's kind of true, but still.

"I'll check. You can come in if you want," I inform as I make enough room for him to enter.

"Nah, I'll just wait here," he says as he hops down from the porch. He immediately begins dribbling the basketball between his legs. I'm still jealous of that. I guess if I'd spend as much time practicing as he does then maybe I'd be able to do that, but art has become my number one. I'm okay with that.

I close the *screen door* and walk to the kitchen where Grandma is. She doesn't like it when we yell from another room if it's as easy as just walking to the next room to talk. That's understandable. She's peeling potatoes over the sink and humming something to herself. I can't quite make it out as it's sort of under her breath. It's completely obvious that Matty got her musical ability passed down from Grandma.   Both of them are always humming or singing something.

"Hey, Grandma?"

"Yeah?" She doesn't look up from the potatoes.

"Can I go to the park and play ball with Bucky and the guys?"

She looks up from her potatoes. I already know what's coming.   She's never let it go that I got into a "physical altercation", as she calls it. She still lets me go to the park from time to time, but there are times that she says no.   I wonder which side of Grandma I'm about to be dealing with. I know that the reasoning in getting me my own basketball goal was partially because I'd have a reason why I didn't need to go to the park anymore.   There are times that the guys come over and we play here, but if we want a bigger game we always go to the park to play. There is always someone there to play ball with.

"Now you promise me that if anything starts getting rowdy that you come straight back. You hear me?"

"Yes ma'am."

"Promise me." She's pointing the potato peeler at me. I better promise!

"I promise."

"Okay. You can go."

She turns back to her potatoes and I turn with a victorious smile toward the screen door. Matty pops her head out the bedroom door as I walk through the living room toward my exit.

"Going to the park?" she asks.
"Wanna come?"
"Randy's coming over soon. Maybe we'll meet you there."
"Okay." I return as I open the door and step onto the porch. Bucky turns as I take the two steps down to where he is. His eyebrows start dancing up and down on his forehead again. There's no way to not smile at that.

We make it to the park and there are enough of us there to play 3 on 3. We play several games before some begin to trickle off and leave. I figure I'll head home as well, maybe see what Matty and Randy are up to since they never made it to the park.

I can hear the piano as I make my way up the drive. Two different things attempting to be played at the same time. It's gotta be Matty and Randy working on their next chart-topping, record-breaking, number one single that will take the world by storm. Just as I finish my thought a couple of chords clash together. Not just oh-that-doesn't-sound-good clash, but almost car wreck sounding. Clearly, they'll have to tighten that up a little before going on tour.

I walk in, and sure enough, Matty and Randy are seated at the piano. I walk over to them.

"Hey!" Randy calls as she punches down a chord.

"You stink!" Matty announces as she looks at me with a scrunched-up nose.

"That's the smell of a Champion Sis!" I grin as I lift my arms. I guess I did work up quite a smell playing the couple of hours we did.

"Well, Champions take showers too you know?" Matty responds. I hug Matty from behind, which launches her into a screaming squirm as she hits my arms. Randy starts laughing at Matty's disgust. The screaming summons Grandma of course. She pokes her head out of the kitchen.

"What's going on out here?" she calls.

"He's so nasty!" Matty yells. She's elbowing and thrashing all the more now.

"I just wanted a hug!" I say with a smile as I release her.

Grandma shakes her head and retreats back into the kitchen. I grab a change of clothes from the bedroom and make my way to the shower. I have to pass back by Matty and Randy as I do, so Matty flinches as I walk by. Of course, I slow my stride to make her think I'm going to grab her again. I nudge Randy with my hip as I pass, which causes her to play some wrong chords.

"Would you just get in there already?" Matty barks.

I laugh as I close the door behind me.

The next few weeks are about the same. Time playing ball with Bucky and Dave. Matty and Randy are inseparable, and I like joining in with them. They like listening to the stereo in the garage when I paint or draw. We all just hang out and have fun. We even get to spend a lot of time with Grandpa and Grandma. It's nice.

At home, it's about the same, but instead of Bucky, Dave, Randy, Grandpa and Grandma, it's Charles, Jason and Mom! Mom's been pretty busy lately, so there hasn't been as much at-home time as there has been time at our Grandparents, but it's still been great. It all feels normal.

So the summer has actually been filled with all the things we love to do. No boredom has had room to set in. If I'm not playing ball, creating art, eating something Grandma made or fixing things with Grandpa, I'm playing Sega, reading comics or just plain hanging out. It's been great! I honestly feel like I'm getting closer to everyone and that feeling of being all alone, that was there not so long ago, is completely gone. My Grandparents are amazing. My friends are amazing. My Mom is amazing. And Matty, my best friend, she's amazing. This has been an amazing summer so far and we're not even halfway through it! AMAZING!

I close the passenger side door behind me as I take a seat and then buckle myself in. Matty's already in the back seat and buckled up. She thinks it's a race every time. She takes pride in being the first one in the car and buckled up. She gets some sort of adrenaline rush every time we go somewhere. I don't know why. No one is ever racing her. I remember racing her so many times before, but it got old. I stopped, she never has. I don't ever say anything. Just let her have it right? She's sort of racing herself. If she ever lost... well that's a weird thought. Anyway!

Mom sits and buckles herself up all in one swoop. She shoots me a wink and then starts the car. The AC is on full blast, as it should be. I position my vent to hit me right in the face. It's not at its max cold yet, but it soon will be and I'm ready to welcome that cool, cool air. Midsummer can be brutal here and if I'm real honest I hate sweating. I don't mind it if I'm playing basketball, because there's a reason to sweat. But if I'm just sitting there and I'm sweating, well that's just stupid.

Mom finds some music on the radio. She lands on GnR (Guns N Roses) which is always acceptable, and then she puts the car in reverse and we back out onto the road. We are headed home. She picked us up early this week. Maybe she got off early?

"What do you guys want to do?" she asks. She adjusts the rearview mirror to better see Matty's face.

"Want to stop off and rent a movie?" she suggests.

"That's fine," Matty responds.

"What about you?" she turns her attention to me.

"Okay. And popcorn?" I respond.

"Yes. And popcorn," Mom answers.

"And candy!" Matty adds.

"Okay, but not too much!" Mom returns with a grin.

"And ice cream," I add.

"And ice cream?" Mom sounds shocked. She's not, just being playful. Plus it would make zero sense if she was shocked that I was suggesting ice cream. "Oh I don't know," she continues.

"Oh it's happenin'," I confidently respond.

"Is it now?" she comes back.

Mom smiles. Sweet Child O' Mine comes to an end. Dang. We talked through the entire song. Bummer. I don't normally like talking through songs. I like to enjoy them. I like to imagine myself as Slash, or Joe Perry, or whoever, playing the guitar solo. I like to imagine myself as the lead singer. Only if I like the song though. Why would I be lead singer of a song that I don't like?

"Okay, so listen guys," Mom starts.

Uh oh. Serious tone...
serious talk table of three!

"We're almost halfway through the summer now. I know that I've been working a lot, but there's something I need to talk to you about."

She pauses for a while. Does she want us to ask? Did she forget what she was going to talk to us about? I know sometimes I start thinking in the middle of something I was saying, and if I allow the thoughts to keep going I totally forget what I was talking about. I try and keep that under control, but it does tend to happen when I get a little too excited about something. Maybe she's got that going on right now?

"I know this last year has been a difficult one," Mom continues.

Okay! She's back!

"I feel like I need to explain myself a little before I continue."

She doesn't have it together. Is she talking to herself now or still talking to us? I'm trying to stay focused, but if she doesn't pull it together soon my mind is going to check out and there's no telling where it'll go.

"People can change. You know what I mean?"
"Like clothes?" Matty responds. "Or transform? Like a werewolf?"
"No, not like a werewolf," Mom sighs.

She's struggling.   That's not normal.   She's usually not at a loss for words, so something's up.   We better not be moving again.   She better not be telling us we're changing addresses or towns or states or continents. I would maybe accept planets. I really just want to know if there are aliens.   I've been watching X-Files, and sometimes it freaks me the crap out, but I love the show! *"I want to believe!"*

"So you know you guys are getting older right?"

> ***Whoa.   Mom.   We're not having THAT conversation. Please do not have THAT conversation with us right now.***

I think the panic of my internal dialogue is on my face because Mom backpedals, with wide eyes as she realizes what I'm thinking.

"I mean, okay. I'm just going to tell you and we can talk it out after okay?"
"Okay Mommy," Matty responds.

Hearing Matty say "Mommy" reminds me that we're still kids.   I forget that when I'm with Mom sometimes. I mean, not literally, because I know we're still kids. It's just we've done a lot of growing up this past year. We're not the same people we were at the beginning of all of this. I understand a lot more. I know a lot more. And Matty, even though she'll lead you to believe otherwise, she's the same way. We're a lot closer now, and in a more grown-up way, I feel. I think at least. Maybe that's what Mom is trying to get at?

"So I need to tell you.   I've been seeing someone."

Mom's been seeing someone.   No childish questions from Matty or myself. We understand what that means.

"You both know him well. He's changed. He's different now."

"Mom," I start, but before I can say anything else she drops the biggest bomb she ever could.

"I've been seeing Chris."

Hello! Mattlock here!

THANK YOU so much for reading GROWING UP:1993!
I would absolutely LOVE to keep in touch with you and hear your thoughts!
Below is a QR code where you can sign up for my emailing list. And YES! It is
actually -ME- that reads and responds.

I don't want you to miss out on any upcoming releases or projects as this is
just Book 1 in a series of several books to come. The story has just begun.

Plus, I'll be releasing extra additional content between books that you'll only
have access to if you've signed up for the emailing list! I really hope I'm
driving the FOMO in deep right now. :)

Talk soon!

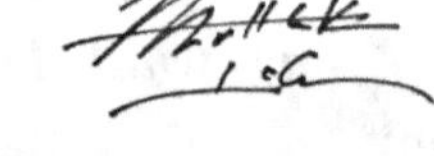

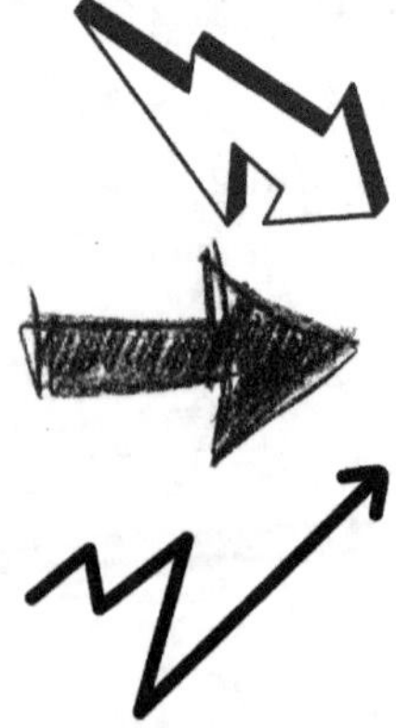

As an author, filmmaker, writer, director, actor and musician, storytelling resonates through everything that Mattlock London does.

Though originally from a small town in Oklahoma named Wagoner, Mattlock has called Maui, Hawaii, Los Angeles, California, Albany, New York, Broken Arrow, and Morris, Oklahoma - among several other places - home. He currently lives in the Dallas metro area in Texas with his wife and three daughters.

Learn more about Mattlock at MATTLOCKLONDON.COM